The
Outsiders

**a full-length play
by
Christopher Sergel**

**based upon the novel
by
S. E. Hinton**

D1533764

The Dramatic Publishing Company
Woodstock, Illinois ● Wilton, Connecticut ● Melbourne, Australia

THE OUTSIDERS

A Full Lenth Play in Two Acts
For 10 or 12 Men and 5 or 7 Women*, Extras

CHARACTERS

PONYBOY ....in his early teens, a greaser
JOHNNY ....Ponyboy's friend, in his early teens
BOB ....a Soc
RANDY .... a Soc
DALLAS ....early 20s, a greaser
TWO-BIT ....early 20s, a greaser
DARRY ....Ponyboy's oldest brother, 20 years old
SODAPOP .. Ponyboy's second oldest brother, mid teens
SANDY ....Sodapop's girlfriend
CHERRY ....a Soc
MARCIA .... Cherry's friend
MRS. O'BRIANT .... a parent
JERRY .... a parent
DOCTOR ....at the hospital
NURSE ....at the hospital
MR. SYME .... an English teacher
PAUL ....early 20s, a Soc

Extras: GREASERS, SOCS, HOSPITAL WORKER,
         CHILDREN (if available)

*If more female roles are desired for your production,
the roles of JERRY and MR. SYME may be played by·
women.

WHAT PEOPLE ARE SAYING about *The Outsiders*...

"Great show! A good challenge for the kids, easy to stage and a lot of fun! Kids love '50s plays." *Lisa Botts, Bolsa Grande High School, Garden Grove, Calif.*

"This piece was beautiful—in the last days of production and the first time I read it, it brought tears to my eyes. The students enjoyed a story with which they were familiar and a script to which they could truly connect." *Shannon Mallrich, Triad High School, Troy, Ill.*

"A beautiful coming-of-age story that any generation can relate to." *Laura LaChappelle, Bradshaw Mountain High School, Humboldt, Ariz.*

ACT ONE

SCENE: *The stage is dark. There's a moment of silence. Then light comes up revealing a young man in the "living area." He is PONYBOY, a young teenager wearing blue jeans and a t-shirt. His hair is long and loaded with hair oil. He's sensitive, insecure and a bit younger than the other young men we'll see. PONYBOY looks for something on the table. Finding a note with a number on it, he dials it on the cradle phone on the table. After a brief pause.*

PONYBOY. Mr. Syme—this is Ponyboy. *(Apologetically in response.)* I didn't realize it was so late. I forgot. *(To the point.)* I'm calling about the theme assignment for English. How long can it be? *(Repeating what he hears.)* Not less than five pages. *(Anxious.)* But can it be longer? Longer than five pages? *(Repeating.)* As long as I want. *(His problem. Apologetically.)* It's all in my head—if I can sort it out. First I have to sort it out. *(Listens. Then nods in agreement.)* As soon as I get it together. No later than that. Thanks, Mr. Syme. *(As he hangs up he's already trying to handle this. He gets up from the table. Deciding on the first step.)* The place to begin—I'd gone to a movie. *(This is a memory. Remembering.)* When I stepped out into the bright sunlight from the darkness of that movie house, I had only two things on my mind: Paul Newman and a ride home.

(General light coming up. PONYBOY blinks his eyes and shakes himself. He's no longer remembering. He's in the present and now he looks directly at the AUDIENCE.)

PONYBOY. I wish I looked like Paul Newman. He looks tough and I don't. *(Traffic sounds are coming up and he considers the imaginary street.)* The other thing—it's a long walk home with no company. But I usually lone it anyway. I like to watch movies undisturbed so I can get into them and live them with the actors. I'm different that way. I mean my second oldest brother, Soda, never cracks a book at all, and my oldest brother, Darry, works too hard to be interested in a story or drawing a picture—so I'm not like them. And nobody in our gang digs movies and books the way I do. So I lone it. *(Sound of a car zooming by and as it does, someone shouts from it.)*

VOICE. Greaser!

PONYBOY *(looks after the car, then front. Defensively).* And I'm a greaser. *(Explaining.)* Greasers can't walk alone too much or they get jumped by the Socs. I'm not sure how you spell that, but it's the abbreviation for the Socials—the jet set, the rich kids. *(There's the sound of a car approaching, driving slowly. PONYBOY notices the sound.)* We're poorer than the Socs. I reckon we're wilder, too. But not like the Socs, who jump greasers and wreck houses and throw beer blasts for kicks. *(Frankly.)* Greasers are almost like hoods; we steal things and drive old souped up cars and have gang fights. I don't mean I do. Darry would kill me if I got in trouble with the police. Since Mom and Dad were killed in a car crash, the three of us get to stay together only as long as we behave. So Soda and I stay out of trouble as much as we can. *(The car has stopped and car doors are opened and then slammed shut. PONYBOY is getting nervous.)* I'm not saying that either the Socs or the greasers are better; that's just the way things are.

(Two young men, RANDY and BOB, obviously "Socials" are entering. RANDY comes on L. PONYBOY turns to start R but BOB enters from that side.)

BOB. Hey, grease —

RANDY. How come you're all by yourself, grease?

PONYBOY *(tightly)*. Stay away from me.

BOB. Couldn't think of it.

RANDY. Not safe for you to be out here all alone.

BOB. We're gonna do you a favor, grease. We're gonna cut off that long greasy hair.

PONYBOY *(tight)*. Leave me alone.

BOB *(pulls a knife and flips open the blade)*. Need a haircut, grease?

PONYBOY *(backing up)*. No. *(BOB advances with the knife.)*

BOB. Gonna cut it real close! How'd you like the haircut to begin just below the chin?

PONYBOY *(panic)*. Are you crazy! *(Shouting.)* Soda! Darry!

BOB. Shut him up.

RANDY. *(looking off L)*. I see someone —

PONYBOY *(frantic)*. Darry!

BOB *(coming at him. Hard)*. Okay, greaser!

RANDY. Cool it, Bob!

BOB *(implacable)*. He's asking —

RANDY *(gestures L)*. Company coming —

BOB *(glancing L. Then to PONYBOY)*. Have to give you another appointment, grease! Catch you later.

(As they hurry along off R, JOHNNY comes rushing on L. He's almost as young as PONYBOY, has a scar on his face and a nervous look that comes from a recent and terrible beating.)

JOHNNY *(frightened)*. Ponyboy! You okay?

(DALLAS is also rushing on followed by TWO-BIT. DAL-LAS is tougher than the rest — tougher, colder, meaner. TWO-BIT is DALLAS's age with a wide grin and always has to get in his "two-bits" — hence his name.)

DALLAS *(to PONYBOY)*. They cut you?

PONYBOY. No. All talk. Nothing.

TWO-BIT *(outraged)*. They're cruising our territory.

DALLAS *(as he starts off R)*. Soc scum! *(DALLAS and TWO-BIT exit.)*

JOHNNY *(concerned)*. You really okay? You're not hurt?

PONYBOY. A little spooked, that's all. *(Looking at JOHNNY.)* Compared to what they did to you — it's nothing. Nothing at all.

JOHNNY *(unhappily)*. They have to stop jumping us! They have to stop.

PONYBOY *(noticing. Concerned)*. What's in your hand?

JOHNNY. It isn't anything. Never mind, Ponyboy.

PONYBOY *(interrupting)*. Johnny — *(JOHNNY lets out a breath. Then he flicks the handle in his hand and the switch blade snaps out.)*

JOHNNY *(softly defensive)*. I can't take another beating —
I can't take it, Ponyboy. *(With a small smile.)* I get
enough from my father.

*(DARRY, followed by SODAPOP, hurries on L.
DARRY's tall and muscular. He looks older than twenty
— tough, cool, smart. SODA is handsome, with a finely-
drawn, sensitive face.)*

DARRY *(anxious)*. Are you all right, Ponyboy? *(Shaking
him.)* Tell me!

PONYBOY. I'm okay. Quit shaking me, Darry, I'm okay.

JOHNNY *(volunteering)*. They didn't cut him.

PONYBOY *(to DARRY who still grips him)*. Come on,
Darry.

DARRY *(lets go and stuffs his hands in his pockets)*.
Sorry.

PONYBOY *(frankly)*. You're never sorry. Not about anything.

SODAPOP. The kid's okay. You're an okay kid, Pony.

(DALLAS and TWO-BIT come back in.)

DARRY. Didya catch 'em?

TWO-BIT. Nup. They got away this time.

DALLAS. I hit their car with a couple rocks. *(With satisfaction.)* I don't think they liked that. *(They're moving
into the living area.)*

PONYBOY. I didn't know you were out of jail, Dallas.

DALLAS. Good behavior. Got off early.

TWO-BIT *(curious)*. Ponyboy, what were you doin' walking by your lonesome?

PONYBOY. I was comin' home from the movies. I didn't think —

DARRY *(breaking in)*. You don't ever think, not at home or anywhere when it counts. You must think at school with all those good grades, and you've always got your nose in a book, but do you ever use your head for common sense? No sirree, bub. And if you had to go by yourself you should've carried a blade.

PONYBOY *(unhappily)*. No matter what I did you wouldn't like it.

SODAPOP. Leave my kid brother alone, you hear? It ain't his fault he likes to go to the movies, and it ain't his fault the Socs like to jump us, and if he'd been carrying a blade it would've been a good excuse to cut him to ribbons.

DARRY *(impatiently)*. When I want my kid brother to tell me what to do with my other kid brother, I'll ask you — kid brother. *(SODAPOP laughs.)*

TWO-BIT. Next time get one of us to go with you, Ponyboy. Any of us will.

DALLAS. Speakin' of movies, I'm walking over to the Nightly Double tomorrow night. Anybody want to come and hunt some action?

DARRY. No time. I'm workin'.

DALLAS. You're *always* workin'.

DARRY *(wryly)*. I've got a choice?

(SANDY is entering L on this. She's pretty, has a soft laugh, and she's a greaser.)

DALLAS. Sodapop?

SODAPOP *(shaking his head)*. I'm picking up Sandy for the game.

SANDY. I'm glad to hear you say that.

SODAPOP *(delighted to see her)*. Sandy! Can you stay?

SANDY *(regretfully)*. No.

SODAPOP *(understanding)*. Things at home? You have to go?

SANDY *(echoing DARRY)*. I've got a choice?

DALLAS *(wanting to get this settled)*. Two-Bit, Johnny-cake, you and Pony wanta come?

PONYBOY. Me and Johnny'll come. Okay, Darry?

SODAPOP *(helpfully)*. It ain't a school night.

DARRY *(agreeing)*. Since it isn't a school night.

TWO-BIT. If I don't get boozed up, I'll walk over and find y'all. *(DALLAS waves and is going off.)*

DARRY *(pointing a warning at PONYBOY)*. If I ever catch *you* getting boozed up —

PONYBOY *(this is unfair)*. Darry! *(But DARRY has gone off into the kitchen.)*

SODAPOP *(laughing)*. Who needs boozed-up?

TWO-BIT *(feeling criticized. To SODAPOP)*. I seen you lotsa times.

PONYBOY *(indignant)*. When?

SANDY *(to PONYBOY, smiling)*. Two-Bit is right. Soda gets drunk lotsa times — at drag races, at a dance, only — he never touches alcohol.

TWO-BIT *(she's crazy)*. C'mon, Sandy.

SANDY *(the whole point)*. He don't need alcohol. *(She looks at him with great affection.)* He gets drunk on just plain living.

TWO-BIT *(they're too much)*. Probably I'll find y'all. *(He's starting to go.)*

JOHNNY *(calling to him. A little anxious)*. Two-Bit — if you're walking toward my place, if you're in that direction, could I — part-way —

TWO-BIT *(considers JOHNNY. Getting his anxiety. Deciding)*. Happens I'll be going right by your place, Johnnycake. Right by your door.

JOHNNY *(with great relief)*. Two-Bit — thanks. *(JOHNNY and TWO-BIT exit.)*

PONYBOY *(looking after them)*. Remember how Johnny looked when he got beat up? Why do the Socs hate us so much?

SANDY *(bitterly)*. That's just how it works. We're greasers.

PONYBOY. I'm reading *Great Expectations* for English, and that kid Pip, he reminds me of us — the way he felt marked lousy because he wasn't a gentleman or anything and the way that girl kept looking down on him.

SODAPOP. That's only a book, Pony.

PONYBOY *(not agreeing)*. It happened to me. One time in biology I had to dissect a worm and the razor wouldn't cut, so I used my switchblade.

SANDY. Pony!

PONYBOY. I forgot what I was doing or I'd never had done it. The minute I flicked it out this girl right beside me kind of gasped and said, "They are right. You are a hood."

SANDY. A Soc? *(PONYBOY nods.)* Was she pretty?

PONYBOY *(nods again)*. She looked real good in yellow. *(Annoyed at himself. To SODAPOP.)* Don't tell Darry. He'll say I didn't think again.

SODAPOP. Probably would, but when he hollers at you — he don't mean nothin'.

PONYBOY. Like hell —

SANDY *(to SODAPOP)*. Have to get home before my mother gets hacked off. *(She's saying "I love you.")* I don't want to miss the game tomorrow.

SODAPOP *(the same in reply)*. Wouldn't miss it for anything. Pick you up at home?

SANDY *(shakes her head quickly)*. Better meet me. I'll be at the Dingo. *(They exchange a smile as she goes.)*

PONYBOY. She's different.

SODAPOP. From what?

PONYBOY. From the only girls that'll look at greasers — tough, loud girls with too much eye make-up, who swear too much. *(Looking after her.)* I like Sandy.

SODAPOP. She doesn't have it easy. She's got school, a job, and nothing but trouble at home.

PONYBOY. Soda?

SODAPOP. Yeah?

PONYBOY. How come you dropped out of school? I could hardly stand it when you left school.

SODAPOP. It's 'cause I'm dumb. The only things I was passing were auto mechanics and gym.

PONYBOY. You're not dumb.

SODAPOP. I am. Shut up and I'll tell you something. Don't tell Darry.

PONYBOY. Okay.

SODAPOP. I think I'm gonna marry Sandy. After she gets out of school and I get a better job and everything. *(Considering PONYBOY.)* I might wait till you get out of school though. So I can help Darry with the bills.

PONYBOY *(approving)*. Tuff enough! *(Then with alarm.)* Only wait till I get out, so you can keep Darry off my back.

SODAPOP *(sharply)*. Don't be like that. I told you he doesn't mean half what he says. He's just got more worries than someone his age ought to. He's really proud of you because you're brainy.

PONYBOY. Sure.

SODAPOP. Maybe we deserve a lot of the trouble we get. Dallas deserves everything he gets and should get worse if you want the truth. And Two-Bit — he doesn't want or need half the things he swipes from stores. *(Strong.)* But it's not like that with Darry. He doesn't deserve to work like an old man when he's only twenty. Even with the athletic scholarships, there wasn't money for college. Darry doesn't go anywhere and he doesn't do anything except work. But he's got hopes for you — you dig?

PONYBOY. Then why does he bug me all the time?

SODAPOP. You're the baby — I mean, he loves you a lot. Savvy?

PONYBOY. You're wrong. Darry don't love anyone or anything. And he thinks I'm just another mouth to feed. That's all I mean to him.

SODAPOP *(quietly)*. You better get on with your homework. *(The light is beginning to dim.)*

PONYBOY *(curious)*. You in love with Sandy?

SODAPOP *(quietly)*. I am.

PONYBOY. What's it like? *(It's almost dark except for the lamp.)*

SODAPOP *(considers. Softly)*. It's real nice. What's that book you're reading for English?

PONYBOY. *Great Expectations.*

SODAPOP *(as he goes off)*. *Great Expectations.*

(PONYBOY looks after SODAPOP wondering what he meant by that. Except for the table lamp the stage is entirely dark. PONYBOY opens up a writing pad and begins to write. In the darkness movie music is heard. During this, two benches are brought in DL diagonally facing the AUDIENCE, one in front of the other. UL the corner

*of a movie popcorn stand is pushed on. PONYBOY is
reading what he's writing.)*

PONYBOY. We were a little early for the movie so we
walked around talking to all the greasers we knew,
leaning in car windows or hopping into back seats, and
getting in on who was running away, and who was in
jail, and who was going with who, and who stole what,
when and why. By then it was dark enough to sneak in
under the back fence of the drive-in.

*(Light is coming up during this on the movie area with
the benches and popcorn stand. Two attractive teenage
girls, CHERRY and MARCIA — both Socs — are coming
on left. They're upset.)*

CHERRY *(turns to shout at someone off L)*. Go home!
Both of you!
MARCIA *(also off L)*. Dry out! *(They come down and sit
in the front row bench facing the AUDIENCE. They're
BOTH angry. DALLAS is seen at the right, impatiently
waving off R.)*
DALLAS *(calling)*. C'mon Johnnycake!

*(JOHNNY comes on and DALLAS gestures at the bot-
tom of an imaginary fence.)*

DALLAS. We'll slide under.
JOHNNY. Why don't we just pay?
DALLAS *(impatient)*. Follow me.

(As JOHNNY follows, sliding under the imaginary fence, PONYBOY has turned out the desk lamp and is coming down to join them.)

PONYBOY *(as he comes).* You know he hates to do things legal.

DALLAS *(calling).* Move it, Ponyboy.

PONYBOY *(following).* Sure, Dallas. *(MARCIA has turned to CHERRY.)*

MARCIA *(she giggles).* You really made them mad.

CHERRY. You object?

MARCIA. Bob and Randy are disgusting. I don't want to sit with them either. *(DALLAS is now observing the GIRLS with interest.)*

CHERRY. They need a lesson. *(Turning front. Emphatically.)* We came to see a movie. We'll see a movie. *(DALLAS is strolling over, followed by the hesitant PONYBOY and JOHNNY.)*

MARCIA *(looking out front at where the screen must be. Reciting the title).* "Bikinis on Muscle Beach."

CHERRY. Must be something by J. D. Salinger.

MARCIA *(seriously).* Really?

CHERRY *(what an idiot).* Marcia! *(DALLAS has seated himself right behind CHERRY while JOHNNY and PONYBOY sit uneasily beside him.)*

DALLAS *(leans over CHERRY's shoulder and looks at the side of her face).* Is this hair real, or a wig? *(CHERRY leans forward away from him. He gives her hair a little tug.)*

CHERRY *(slaps his hand away).* Stop that.

DALLAS. I guess it's real. *(Suggestively.)* Wanta check if I'm real?

PONYBOY *(a faint protest).* Dallas –

MARCIA. Watch the picture.

DALLAS. "Bikinis on Muscle Beach" — *(He puts his feet up on the bench beside CHERRY.)* Like to see some muscle?

CHERRY *(sharply)*. Take your feet off my seat and shut up!

DALLAS *(looking at the sky. Amused)*. Who's gonna make me?

MARCIA *(has looked at them and turns to CHERRY)*. That's the greaser that jockeys for the Slash J sometimes.

DALLAS. I know you two. I've seen you around rodeos.

CHERRY *(coolly)*. It's a shame you can't *ride* bull half as good as you can talk it.

DALLAS. You two barrel race, huh?

CHERRY. You'd better leave us alone — or I'll call the cops.

DALLAS *(bored out of his mind)*. Oh, my, my — you've got me scared to death! You ought to see my record sometime, baby. *(Grinning slyly.)* Guess what I've been in for?

CHERRY. *Please* leave us alone. Why don't you be nice and leave us alone?

DALLAS. I'm never nice. Want a Coke?

CHERRY. I wouldn't drink it if I was starving in the desert. *(Over her shoulder.)* Get lost, hood! *(DALLAS shrugs and strolls off toward the popcorn stand. CHERRY glares at PONYBOY.)* Are you going to start on us?

PONYBOY *(sincerely)*. No.

CHERRY *(suddenly she smiles)*. You don't look the type. What's your name?

PONYBOY. I wish you hadn't asked. It's — Ponyboy Curtis.

CHERRY *(smiling)*. That's an original and lovely name.

PONYBOY *(pleased)*. My dad was an original person. I've got a brother named Sodapop and it says so on his birth certificate.

CHERRY. My name's Sherrie, but I'm called Cherry because of my hair. Cherry Valance.

PONYBOY. I know. You're a cheerleader. We go to the same school.

MARCIA. You don't look old enough for high school.

PONYBOY. I'm not. I got put up a year in grade school.

CHERRY. What's a nice, smart kid like you running around with trash like that for?

PONYBOY *(stiffly)*. I'm a grease, same as Dallas. He's my buddy.

CHERRY *(softly)*. I'm sorry, Ponyboy. *(Then curious.)* Your brother Sodapop, does he work in a gasoline station? A DX?

PONYBOY. Yeah.

CHERRY. Man, your brother is one doll. I might've guessed you were brothers—you look alike. *(As PONY-BOY grins.)* How come you're blushing?

JOHNNY. It's not every day I hear a good looking Soc say something like that.

MARCIA. How come we don't see him in school?

PONYBOY *(winces)*. He's a dropout.

(DALLAS is coming back with some Cokes.)

DALLAS *(handing out Cokes)*. Johnnycake, Pony—*(Then handing one to MARCIA.)* For you. *(With insinuation.)* For the redhead who likes muscles. *(DALLAS sits down beside her.)* Might cool you off.

CHERRY *(gives him an incredulous look. Then she sloshes the Coke in his face)*. This might cool you off, greaser. After you wash your mouth and learn to talk and act decent, I might cool off, too. *(PONYBOY and JOHNNY are stunned and fearful of an explosion. DALLAS wipes the Coke off his face with his sleeve and smiles dangerously at CHERRY.)*

DALLAS *(aggressive)*. Fiery, huh? *(Starting to put his arm around her.)* Well that's the way I like 'em. *(JOHNNY has been upset by this and he stands up suddenly.)*

JOHNNY *(blurts out)*. Leave her alone, Dallas. *(DALLAS is completely startled by this from JOHNNY.)*

DALLAS. Huh? *(With disbelief.)* What'd you say, Johnny-cake?

JOHNNY *(gulps hard)*. You heard me. Leave her alone. *(DALLAS is outraged and jumps up whirling to confront JOHNNY.)*

DALLAS *(furious)*. Johnny! You want to repeat that?

JOHNNY *(terrified but not budging. Closing his eyes tight. A desperate whisper)*. Leave her alone. *(DALLAS's impulse is to belt him, but he can't. JOHNNY's his pet. DALLAS forces himself to jam his fists in his pockets. Then he turns abruptly and stalks off. As DALLAS goes, JOHNNY lets out the breath he's been holding.)*

CHERRY *(also relaxing. To JOHNNY)*. Thanks. He had me scared.

JOHNNY *(managing a smile)*. You sure didn't show it. *(Emphatically.)* Nobody talks to Dallas like you did.

CHERRY. From what I saw, you do.

PONYBOY. One time a guy told Dallas to move over at a candy counter and Dallas belted him so hard it knocked a tooth loose. *(Incredulous.)* You gotta lot of guts, Johnny.

JOHNNY *(embarrassed)*. Will you cool it, Ponyboy?

MARCIA. Y'all sit up here with us. You can protect us.

JOHNNY. Okay.

PONYBOY. Might as well. *(As they're sitting on the front bench.)*

MARCIA. How old are y'all?

PONYBOY. Fourteen.

JOHNNY. Sixteen.

MARCIA. That's funny. I thought you were both—

CHERRY *(cutting in. Tactfully)*. Sixteen.

JOHNNY *(smiling)*. How come y'all ain't scared of us like you were Dallas?

CHERRY *(sighs)*. First, you didn't join in the way Dallas was talking. Then you made him leave us alone. And when we asked you to sit up here, you didn't act like it was an invitation to make out for the night.

JOHNNY *(considering all this)*. Oh.

CHERRY. I've heard about Dallas Winston, and he looks mean. *(Looking them over.)* But not you two.

PONYBOY. Sure—we're young and innocent.

CHERRY *(looking at PONYBOY carefully)*. No—not innocent. You've seen too much to be innocent. Just not —dirty.

JOHNNY. Dallas's okay. He's tough, but he's a cool old guy.

PONYBOY. He'd leave you alone if he knew you.

MARCIA. We'll I'm glad he doesn't know us.

CHERRY *(half to herself)*. It's funny—in a way I kind of admire him.

PONYBOY *(curious)*. Weren't you yellin' at someone a while ago?

MARCIA. Our dates. They brought along some booze.

CHERRY. I don't want to sit in a drive-in and watch someone get drunk.

MARCIA *(to CHERRY)*. You *really* made 'em mad.

CHERRY. I don't care.

(TWO-BIT has entered during this, coming up behind JOHNNY and PONYBOY. Now he puts a heavy hand on JOHNNY's shoulder, and the other on PONYBOY's shoulder.)

TWO-BIT *(in a deep threatening voice)*. Okay, greasers, you've had it. *(Both PONYBOY and JOHNNY gasp.)*

PONYBOY *(looking up. Relaxing)*. Glory, Two-Bit—you want to scare us to death? We—*(He stops as he looks at JOHNNY whose eyes are shut and he's shaking hard. Concerned.)* Johnny—

TWO-BIT *(realizing)*. Kid—*(Encouraging.)* Johnny—c'mon!

JOHNNY *(has opened his eyes and looks up. Weakly)*. Hey, Two-Bit.

TWO-BIT *(genuinely contrite)*. Sorry, kid. *(Messes JOHNNY's hair.)* I forgot. *(He climbs over to sit by MARCIA.)* Who's this, your great aunts?

MARCIA. Great grandmothers twice removed.

TWO-BIT. A sharp one. How could you two be picked up by a couple of greasy hoods like Pony and Johnny?

MARCIA. We really picked them up. We're Arabian slave traders and we're thinking about shanghaiing them. They're worth ten camels apiece.

TWO-BIT. Five. They don't talk Arabian. Say something in Arabian, Johnnycake.

JOHNNY *(embarrassed)*. Cut it out, Two-Bit. Dallas was bothering them, and when he left they wanted us to sit with them—to protect them against greasers like you.

TWO-BIT. Where is ol' Dallas? Tim Shepherd is looking for him.

PONYBOY. Dallas's huntin' some action.

TWO-BIT. He'll probably find a fight. He slashed the tires on Tim's car just for kicks—which is no joke when you've got to work to pay for them. *(Shrugs.)* So they have a fight.

CHERRY. You don't believe in playing rough or anything.

TWO-BIT. Tim's okay. A fair fight isn't rough. Blades are rough. So are chains and heaters and pool sticks. Skin fighting ain't rough. *(The way it is.)* Dallas got caught. He pays up. No sweat.

CHERRY *(sarcastically)*. Yeah, boy. Real simple.

MARCIA. If he gets killed or something, you just bury him. No sweat.

TWO-BIT *(grinning)*. You dig okay, baby.

CHERRY *(she's upset)*. Ponyboy, will you come with me? We'll get some popcorn?

PONYBOY *(jumping up)*. Sure. Y'all want some?

CHERRY *(cutting this off)*. Y'all watch the movie. *(To PONYBOY.)* C'mon. *(As she leads PONYBOY right, the light on the bench area is dimming.)*

TWO-BIT *(to MARCIA)*. I don't think I have your numbers.

MARCIA. What numbers?

TWO-BIT. Street address and telephone. *(MARCIA is startled by this and JOHNNY is leaning into their exchange. To JOHNNY, faintly annoyed).* The girl said you should watch the movie. So watch the movie. *(JOHNNY quickly turns toward the imaginary screen. MARCIA starts looking through her pocket.)*

MARCIA. Maybe I have a piece of paper somewhere—

(The light has dimmed on the bench area. CHERRY has gone down R where she stands in a bit of light, perplexed by a lot of new thought. PONYBOY has paused half-way in between. He's looking off over the AUDIENCE. For the moment, he's looking back on this.)

PONYBOY *(as he recalls it)*. Cherry didn't really want popcorn. She wanted to talk.

CHERRY *(calls to PONYBOY)*. Your friend—the one with the sideburns—he's okay?

PONYBOY *(crossing to CHERRY)*. He ain't dangerous like Dallas if that's what you mean. He's okay.

CHERRY. Johnny's been hurt bad sometimes, hasn't he? Hurt and scared.

PONYBOY. Worse than that *(Uneasily.)* It was the Socs.

CHERRY *(with decision)*. I don't want to watch "Bikinis on Muscle Beach." I want to know about this. *(PONYBOY considers for an instant, then decides to tell her. It's difficult and painful for him.)*

PONYBOY. Soda and I were kicking rocks down the street and we noticed Johnny's jacket on the ground. Then we saw a hump the other side of the lot. And there was a moan. Soda got there first, and turned him over. *(Has to pause.)* I nearly puked. *(Continues with difficulty.)* We're used to seeing Johnny banged up— his father clobbers him a lot. *(With horror.)* But nothing like this. *(Has to take a breath.)* Soda was on his knees holding him, his body all limp, giving him little shakes, saying, "It's okay, Johnnycake. They're gone now. It's okay." *(It's vivid in his mind.)* Two-Bit was suddenly there, and for once he had nothing smart to say. Dallas got there, too, swearing under his breath, then turning away, and he was sick. Dallas! Finally

Johnny figured it was Soda holding him. He started shaking and crying—couldn't stop himself. He said there was a whole bunch—a blue Mustang full. Soda kept holding him saying, "Don't talk," and over and over, "They've gone. They've gone, Johnnycake."

CHERRY *(cautiously)*. A blue Mustang?

PONYBOY *(nods again)*. Johnny tried to run, but they caught him. One of them had rings on his hand. That's what cut Johnny so bad.

CHERRY *(disturbed)*. All Socs aren't like that. You have to believe me, Ponyboy. Not all of us are like that.

PONYBOY. Sure.

CHERRY. That's like saying all greasers are like Dallas Winston. I bet he's jumped a few people.

PONYBOY *(conceding, nods)*. Lotsa times.

CHERRY. You think the Socs have it made, don't you?

PONYBOY *(sharply)*. Well you do.

CHERRY. It may come as a surprise, but we have troubles you've never even heard of. You want to know something. Things are tough all over.

PONYBOY. Then why are we so different?

CHERRY *(considering)*. You're more emotional. We're sophisticated—cool to the point of not feeling anything. I'll catch myself talking and realize I don't mean half what I'm saying. I don't really think a beer blast on the river bottom is super-cool, but I'll rave about it just to be saying something. *(She suddenly smiles at him.)* I've never told that to anyone. You're the first person. *(Truly curious.)* Why is that?

PONYBOY *(wryly)*. Because I'm a greaser and because I'm younger. So you don't have to keep your guard up.

CHERRY *(admiring)*. For a kid, you're awful smart.

PONYBOY. Probably I'll outgrow it. *(Nods left.)* We'd better buy some popcorn and get back. *(Movie music is climaxing and then ends.)*

CHERRY *(glances at the imaginary screen)*. The picture's ending. *(Curiously.)* You read a lot, don't you, Pony-boy?

PONYBOY. Yeah. Why?

CHERRY. I could just tell. And I bet you watch sunsets. *(PONY nods.)* I used to watch them, too, before I got so busy.

(MARCIA, TWO-BIT and JOHNNY are coming across toward them.)

TWO-BIT. You eat all the popcorn?

CHERRY. It was delicious.

MARCIA *(to CHERRY)*. How'll we get home? Maybe I should call my folks.

TWO-BIT *(gallantly)*. I'll walk you.

MARCIA. It's twenty miles.

JOHNNY *(seriously)*. It's still early and if we get started right away —

TWO-BIT *(be realistic)*. Johnny. *(To the GIRLS.)* There's a car at my place. Take us ten minutes to walk there — *(CHERRY and MARCIA look at each other uncertainly.)* It runs real good. *(A little lame as they don't respond.)* I could drive you —

PONYBOY *(to CHERRY, teasing her)*. Tryin' to figure what's the cool thing to do?

CHERRY *(to PONYBOY)*. Two-Bit's car is okay?

PONYBOY. It's a wreck, but Two-Bit'll get you home.

CHERRY *(deciding)*. Thanks, Two-Bit. Let's start walking.

MARCIA *(aside to CHERRY)*. Aren't we adventurous —

CHERRY. If you'd rather call your parents—

MARCIA *(after considering for one second)*. Nah. *(TWO-BIT points forward, and they start a slow in-place walk.)*

TWO-BIT. Maybe I should run ahead and clean out the back seat.

CHERRY. We'll walk together.

TWO-BIT *(trying to remember. Half to himself)*. I'm sure there's enough gas.

MARCIA *(noticing out left)*. Cherry, look what's coming. *(They ALL look out left.)*

TWO-BIT *(admiring)*. Man, that's a tuff car! Mustangs are tuff!

MARCIA. What are we gonna do?

CHERRY. Stand here. There isn't much else we can do. *(Sound of a car approaching.)*

TWO-BIT. Who is it? The F.B.I.?

CHERRY *(bleakly)*. It's Randy and Bob. *(The sound is passing and their heads turn together as the car evidently goes by.)*

TWO-BIT. And a few more of the socially elite checkered shirt set in the back seat.

JOHNNY *(keeping himself in control)*. Your boyfriends?

CHERRY. Maybe they didn't see us. Act normal.

TWO-BIT. Who's acting. I'm a natural normal.

PONYBOY. Wish it was the other way around.

TWO-BIT. You mean—*(Not sure whether or not this is an insult.)* Whata ya mean?

MARCIA *(with relief)*. That was close. *(JOHNNY has been standing frozen. CHERRY notices JOHNNY.)*

JOHNNY *(starting to shake a little)*. It's—

CHERRY. What?

JOHNNY. Blue.

MARCIA. What is — *(He's still looking after the car. CHERRY looks where he's looking and then back to JOHNNY.)*

CHERRY *(trying to divert him)*. Tell me, Johnny — *(Reaching for his attention.)* Why do they call you Johnny-cake?

TWO-BIT. Real name's Johnny Cade. So everyone —

PONYBOY *(apprehensively)*. They have to get home. *(Prodding.)* Gotta move it, Johnny. *(As they start walking in place again, CHERRY is concerned about JOHNNY and trying to find a way to help.)*

CHERRY. Johnny — what does it mean when you say, "tuff"? It's a "tuff" car?

TWO-BIT. It means —

CHERRY. I was asking Johnny.

JOHNNY *(forced to comment)*. It means okay — really right — sharp. *(With a sly smile now.)* Like you and Marcia are two tuff girls.

CHERRY. Do you have brothers at home to help with things?

JOHNNY *(shakes his head)*. No. Ponyboy's lucky. He's got two.

PONYBOY *(correcting)*. I'm lucky to have Sodapop.

JOHNNY. And Darry.

PONYBOY *(annoyed)*. Are you crazy?

CHERRY. You don't talk about your oldest brother.

PONYBOY. What's to talk about? He's big and handsome and he used to play football.

CHERRY. That's it? Tell me what he's like.

JOHNNY. He's a good guy.

PONYBOY *(to JOHNNY)*. You're completely — *(He turns to CHERRY.)* He's hard as a rock and about as human.

He's got eyes exactly like frozen ice. He thinks I'm a pain in the neck, and he can't stand me.

TWO-BIT *(disagreeing)*. Hold on—

JOHNNY. You and Darry—

PONYBOY *(a cry)*. It's true. I bet he wishes he could stick me in a home somewhere, and he'd do it, too, if Soda'd let him.

TWO-BIT. That ain't right, Ponyboy.

JOHNNY. You got it all wrong. Darry really cares about you.

PONYBOY. You just shut up, Johnny Cade. Darry don't want me at home. *(Accusing.)* And we all know you ain't wanted at home either. *(JOHNNY winces at this and starts to shake again.)*

TWO-BIT *(furious. He punches JOHNNY's shoulder)*. How could you talk to Johnny like that? How could you do it? *(Puts a protective hand on JOHNNY's shoulder.)* He didn't mean it, Johnny.

PONYBOY *(horrified and miserable)*. I'm sorry. I was just mad—'cause I was makin' a fool of myself in front of everybody.

JOHNNY. It's the truth. I ain't wanted. And I don't care.

TWO-BIT *(messing JOHNNY's hair)*. Shut up talkin' like that. We couldn't get along without you.

MARCIA *(uncomfortable. To CHERRY)*. Maybe I should call for a ride.

PONYBOY *(his voice hushed with passion)*. It just don't seem fair.

CHERRY. What isn't fair?

PONYBOY. Like—Johnny's father being a mean drunk and his mother a selfish slob. Two-Bit's mother working in a bar to support him and his kid sister after his father ran out on them. And Dallas—he hates the world. *(He has to catch his breath.)* Even Sodapop—a dropout so he could get a job and keep me in school. Then Darry—getting old before his time trying to run a family and hang on to two jobs and never having any fun. *(Confronting CHERRY and MARCIA.)* While the Socs have so much spare time and money they gang up on us and jump each other just for kicks. They have beer blasts and river bottom parties because they don't know what else to do.

CHERRY. I tried to explain.

PONYBOY. Sure. Things are rough all over. All over our part of town. *(There's the sound of a car suddenly approaching and stopping short.)*

TWO-BIT *(during the above)*. The way things are. Like it or lump it. *(CHERRY and MARCIA staring right.)*

CHERRY *(resigned)*. They've spotted us.

TWO-BIT *(seeing it)*. The blue Mustang.

(BOB and RANDY are coming in R. They don't seem to see the GREASERS.)

BOB. Cherry, Marcia, listen to us—

RANDY. You're making a big deal out of nothing.

BOB. Because we got a little drunk—

CHERRY *(mad)*. A little? You call reeling and passing out in the street "a little"?

BOB. Now look—

CHERRY. No, you look. I told you I'm never going out with you while you're drinking. Too many things could happen.

BOB. Baby, you know we don't get drunk very often.

CHERRY. You're not hearing very good. I said *never!*

RANDY *(reasoning)*. Cherry—Marcia—

BOB. And even if you're mad at us, that's no reason to be walking with these —

PONYBOY. These what?

BOB. Vermin. *(This is the challenge and EVERYONE tightens up.)*

PONYBOY. Who you callin' vermin?

BOB *(to RANDY)*. This is the little grease that needs a haircut.

PONYBOY *(tightly)*. And this is the Soc with the blue Mustang — *(Noticing.)* And all the rings on his hand —

BOB *(menacing with his fist)*. Maybe you'd like a close look —

CHERRY *(hushed)*. It *was* you.

MARCIA. Cool off, guys.

BOB. You greasers think you can pick up our girls? *Our* girls!

TWO-BIT. You're outa your territory. You better watch it.

BOB. Next time pick your own kind — dirt. *(TWO-BIT and PONYBOY tense up.)*

RANDY. Listen, greasers, we got four more in the back seat.

TWO-BIT *(looking at the sky)*. Then pity the back seat.

RANDY. If you're looking for a fight —

JOHNNY *(hushed to PONYBOY. Terrified)*. Should we run for it?

PONYBOY *(aside to him)*. Too late.

RANDY. Hey, I asked you —

TWO-BIT. You mean if I'm looking for a good jumping, you outnumber us, so you'll give it to us.

RANDY *(shouts back to car)*. Hey —

BOB *(to TWO-BIT)*. You got it right. *(At JOHNNY, contemptuously.)* Okay kid, you want a repeat performance?

CHERRY *(a fury. To BOB)*. You touch that kid, I'll call the police. *(BOB and RANDY are stunned.)*

RANDY. Hold it a minute.

BOB. You'll *what?*

MARCIA. Back off, guys.

BOB *(to CHERRY)*. You wouldn't dare.

CHERRY. I don't want a fight. So we'll ride home with you. But *first* — you go sit in the car and you wait.

BOB. Wait?

CHERRY. You wait till we come over.

TWO-BIT *(to CHERRY)*. Hey. We ain't scared of them.

CHERRY. I can't stand fights — I can't stand them. *(To BOB.)* Yes or no?

BOB *(conceding)*. We'll wait one minute. *(To PONY-BOY.)* You think I'll let a little grease get away with walking *my* girl?

CHERRY. Bob, wait in the car. *(Stares at them.)* I said I'll be along in a minute.

BOB *(he's going. Back to PONYBOY. Threatening)*. See ya —

CHERRY *(turns to PONYBOY)*. We'd better go with them, Ponyboy.

PONYBOY. I know —

CHERRY *(uncomfortable)*. It's too dangerous. If I see you in the hall at school and don't say hi, it's not personal. It's —

PONYBOY *(filling in for her)*. The way things are.

CHERRY *(perplexed)*. We couldn't even let our parents see us with you.

PONYBOY. It's okay. Just don't forget, some of us watch sunsets, too. *(Moment of silence as they look at each other.)*

MARCIA *(warning CHERRY)*. Let's not push the one minute warning.

CHERRY *(agreeing)*. It's time. *(She waves at the OTH-ERS, then speaks to PONYBOY.)* I hope I never see that Dallas Winston again.

PONYBOY *(with an edge)*. Because he's one of us?

CHERRY *(just for PONYBOY)*. Because I might fall in love with him. *(A smile as she goes.)* How'd that be for trouble? *(CHERRY and MARCIA are gone. PONY-BOY, JOHNNY and TWO-BIT look after them as the sound of a car pulling away fades. TWO-BIT tears up a bit of paper he's holding.)*

TWO-BIT *(as PONYBOY looks at him)*. Marcia's phone number. I musta been outa my mind to ask for it. Probably phony anyway. *(Giving himself a shake.)* Think I'll go play a little snooker or hunt up a poker game. I dunno — *(Glances off again.)* Those two girls were tuff!

PONYBOY. But if they see us in school, they can't say hi.

TWO-BIT *(as he goes. Sarcastic)*. If that's your worst problem — *(Lights begin to dim.)*

JOHNNY *(defending them)*. They saved us from a fight, Pony. *(Takes a quick breath.)* I'm really glad we didn't have to fight.

PONYBOY. We'd a done okay.

JOHNNY *(his voice rising)*. You don't understand. I couldn't take it again. I'd rather kill myself or something.

PONYBOY *(sharply)*. You can't kill yourself. Don't talk like that. *(They're now in dim moonlight.)*

JOHNNY. I gotta do something. *(Unhappily.)* Maybe I'll sleep here in the park tonight. Listen to the water in the little fountain. Pretend it's a waterfall some place in the mountains. *(As he considers the sky.)* There oughta be someplace without greasers or Socs — with just people. *(Note: In the dark a small fountain may have been pushed just onstage left. If this isn't practical then JOHNNY can imagine it just off left.)*

PONYBOY. Maybe out in the country. When we had the whole family, we'd drive out in the country.

JOHNNY. Lemme tell you something crazy. I think I like it better when the old man's hittin' me. *(Sighs.)* At least then I know he knows who I am. *(Staring into the night.)* I walk in that house and nobody says anything. I walk out, nobody says anything. I stay away all night and nobody notices. *(To PONYBOY.)* At least you got Soda. I ain't got nobody.

PONYBOY. Shoot, you got the whole gang.

JOHNNY. Not like having your own folks care about you. *(He lies back and speaks softly to the sky.)* It ain't the same. *(PONYBOY looks over to where JOHNNY has curled up, then comes down a few steps, standing in a bit of moonlight.)*

PONYBOY. Johnny went to sleep right away. Since I was asleep, too, and dreaming, I brought Mom and Dad back to life. Mom'd bake things and Dad would drive the pick-up out early to feed cattle. *(Visualizing.)* My mom was golden and beautiful — *(His tone changes. He's no longer remembering a dream.)* When I woke up, I thought, "Glory, what time is it?" *(After a quick look.)* Johnny was still asleep. *(Beginning to get urgent.)* Just thinking about facing Darry this late made me shake. I ran home and when I got close I could see —

(PONYBOY looks toward the living area. A shielded light above the living area comes on, as does a lamp inside. DARRY is sitting in a chair reading, and SODA-POP is stretched out on a cot.)

PONYBOY. If only they're asleep. *(PONYBOY is cautiously opening the imaginary door.)*

DARRY *(as he does)*. Pony! *(PONYBOY comes in, swallowing hard. DARRY throws down the paper and jumps up. SODAPOP is stirring on the cot. DARRY is furious.)* Where the heck have you been? *(PONYBOY is too frightened to reply.)* Do you know what time it is? *(PONYBOY shakes his head.)* Well it's two in the morning, kiddo. Another hour and I would have had the police out after you. *(His voice rising.)* Where were you? *Where in the almighty universe were you?*

PONYBOY *(shakily)*. I — I went to sleep in the lot.

DARRY *(shouting)*. You what? *(SODAPOP is sitting up.)*

SODAPOP. Hey, Ponyboy, where ya been?

PONYBOY *(pleading)*. I didn't mean to. I was talkin' to Johnny and we both dropped off.

DARRY. It never occurred to you that your brothers might be worrying their heads off and afraid to call the police because it might get you thrown in a boys' home so quickly it'd make your head spin — and you're asleep in the lot! *(Outraged.)* What's the matter with you?

PONYBOY *(frustrated and getting as furious as DARRY)*. I said I didn't mean to!

DARRY *(shouting back, even louder)*. I didn't mean to! I didn't think! I forgot! That's all I hear out of you. *(Exploding.)* Can't you think of anything?

SODAPOP. Darry, hey — *(Reasoning.)* Darry —

DARRY *(turning his anger on SODAPOP)*. You keep your smart mouth shut! I'm sick and tired of hearing you stick up for him.

PONYBOY *(this is too much)*. Don't yell at him! *(Pulling at DARRY. At this, DARRY wheels around and slaps PONYBOY on the side of his head. PONYBOY staggers back, stunned. SODAPOP is heartbroken. There's a moment of deathly quiet. DARRY looks at the palm of his hand and then back to PONYBOY.)*

DARRY *(a plea)*. Ponyboy. *(PONYBOY gasps, turns and rushes out the door, and as he goes out the light in the living area and over the porch are dimming. As the light goes out, a cry after PONYBOY.)* I didn't mean to! Pony! *(PONYBOY moves right then left, then comes to a stop in the dim moonlight.)*

PONYBOY. I remember — my first thought. I'll find Johnny and we'll run away. I remember — I thought — at least things can't get worse. *(The rumble of a drum begins.)* I was wrong. *(Calls.)* Johnny!

JOHNNY *(from darkness)*. By the fountain, Pony! Watch out!

SOC VOICE *(from darkness, L)*. Here they are, guys!

PONYBOY *(not able to see. Worried)*. What's wrong?

SOC VOICE. Get 'em! Grab the one by the fountain. Got ya!

JOHNNY *(terrified)*. Cut it out. *(Drums are much louder. Then JOHNNY cries out in pain.)*

PONYBOY *(plunging into darkness at left)*. Johnny! *(All lights are now out.)*

SOC VOICE. Start off giving this one a bath!

PONYBOY. Let go!

BOB'S VOICE. Take a drink, greaser!

PONYBOY *(gasps. Choking)*. No! Stop!

JOHNNY *(frantic)*. Let him breathe! He'll drown.

PONYBOY *(a quick gasp)*. Help me, Johnnycake!

BOB'S VOICE. This time you stay down, grease!

JOHNNY *(desperately)*. He's drowning! He'll die! *(Drums to maximum. Suddenly a bright spot illuminates BOB. He's DC, his fists clenched with the rows of rings flashing in the light. His mouth is pulled back tight in a grimace showing his clenched teeth. His body is rigid. The instant is held in the bright light, with the drum pounding. BOB lets out a piercing scream and collapses to the ground. Drums stop. Lights out. Total silence.)*

PONYBOY *(still choking).* Johnny — Johnny — *(Cool moonlight illuminates the stage. BOB is sprawled out on the ground. He's dead. JOHNNY is sitting, one elbow on his knee, staring at nothing. PONYBOY, his face and hair soaking wet, is trying to collect himself. In a low voice.)* What happened?

JOHNNY *(slowly).* I killed him. I killed him. *(They BOTH look at BOB. JOHNNY shows PONYBOY the switch-blade, then closes it.)*

PONYBOY. I think I'm gonna be sick.

JOHNNY *(quietly).* Go ahead. I already was.

PONYBOY *(closes his eyes).* This can't be happening. This can't be — *(To JOHNNY. Incredulous.)* You killed him?

JOHNNY. They were about to drown you. You were about to die. *(Seeing it again.)* They all ran when I stabbed him.

PONYBOY *(the full horror beginning to hit him).* They put you in the electric chair for killing people. *(Helpless.)* What are we gonna do?

JOHNNY. I don't know.

(DALLAS is coming quietly out of the darkness.)

DALLAS *(in a low voice).* First thing — keep your mouths shut.

PONYBOY. Dallas —

DALLAS *(taking everything in)*. I heard the Socs were cruising our neighborhood.

JOHNNY. They were killing Ponyboy—*(They look at BOB.)* So I—

DALLAS. I see. *(Looks off, then back.)* The police'll be here any minute. You need money and you need a plan. *(To PONYBOY.)* Darry and Sodapop know about this? *(PONYBOY shakes his head.)* Boy howdy, I ain't itchin' to be the one to tell Darry.

PONYBOY. Don't tell him.

DALLAS *(handing PONYBOY his jacket)*. Put this on or you die of pneumonia 'fore the cops get you. There's fifty bucks in the pocket.

JOHNNY. What do we do?

DALLAS *(all business)*. Hop the three-fifteen freight to Windrixville. There's an abandoned church on top of Jay Mountain with a pump in the back, so don't worry about water. Buy a supply of food as soon as you get there—*this* morning before the story gets out. Then don't stick your noses out till I come. *(Glances at his watch.)* Git goin'.

JOHNNY. Dallas—thanks.

DALLAS *(wryly)*. I thought New York was the only place I could get mixed up in a murder rap.

PONYBOY. Murder rap?

DALLAS *(urgently)*. I said—*git goin'!* *(They scurry off. DALLAS looks over at the dead BOB. There's a final crashing drumbeat.)*

BLACKOUT

ACT TWO

SCENE: *In the darkness there's the sound of a train whistle. As the light comes up, PONYBOY and JOHNNY are DL looking out over the AUDIENCE. At the right there's a flat of some old boards, a section of an old wooden church partway on stage.*

PONYBOY. Beginning to get light.

JOHNNY *(looking R)*. The old church is over there. Dallas was right.

PONYBOY *(wryly)*. My dream's come true. We're in the country.

JOHNNY. You wait at the church. I'll go to the store for supplies. Be there first thing when they open.

PONYBOY. I wonder what's happening with the guys back home?

JOHNNY *(nervously. As he goes)*. I can imagine.

PONYBOY. I can imagine, too. *(JOHNNY is gone. PONYBOY turns and is crossing R as the light comes up in the living area. He pauses before going off)*. Later we found out.

(Light is up on the living area revealing DARRY and SODAPOP standing there looking out.)

SODAPOP. Maybe Dallas knows something.

DARRY. He didn't say.

SODAPOP. But maybe he knows somethin'. When the police worked him over he told them he thought they were headed for Texas.

DARRY *(wondering)*. Do you think maybe —

SODAPOP *(emphatic)*. One thing sure. They're *not* headed for Texas.

DARRY. First time I've missed work since —

SODAPOP. If you wanta go on in — *(He's stopped by a hard look from DARRY.)*

DARRY. Maybe this time he'll think to give us a phone call.

SODAPOP. If there's a phone handy, and if he has some money, and if nobody is around, and if —

DARRY *(enough)*. Okay.

(SANDY is coming in L.)

SANDY *(one glance is enough)*. No news. *(As she looks at them.)* You both been up all night.

SODAPOP *(shrugs)*. How'd you make out at home?

SANDY. Not good. The worst.

SODAPOP. That bad?

SANDY. I said — the worst. *(She has bad news.)* We have to talk.

SODAPOP *(as he considers her)*. I'm getting a little nervous.

SANDY. I can't live at home anymore. I have to get out — right now.

DARRY *(leaving them alone)*. C'n always stay here, Sandy. *(He's gone.)*

SODAPOP *(bewildered)*. How can you get out — *right now?*

SANDY. How can I stay? *(She takes a breath.)* I've been up all night, too.

SODAPOP. You shoulda called.

SANDY *(this is it)*. Sodapop—I'm going to Tallahassee, Florida. My grandmother lives there. I'm gonna live with my grandmother in Florida.

SODAPOP. Hold on! You don't have to do that. You could stay here. You heard Darry. You don't have to go to Florida.

SANDY. I can't stay here.

SODAPOP. We could get married. We're gonna some-day, so why not—

SANDY *(no hope)*. We're sixteen.

SODAPOP. A couple weeks I'll be seventeen.

SANDY. Big difference.

SODAPOP. No, Sandy. I'll be—I won't—

SANDY. I have to get away. I can't talk about it anymore. *(She takes a breath.)* And—I can't see you anymore.

SODAPOP *(stunned)*. What?

SANDY. That's what I came to tell you. *(As SODAPOP starts to say something, she puts a hand over his mouth.)* It's hard enough, Sodapop.

SODAPOP. But—

SANDY *(a plea)*. Don't make it worse. *(Begging.)* Don't do that.

SODAPOP *(grabs a breath)*. Okay. Okay—for now. It's been a bad night. You have to back off for a while. Okay. But we'll write. Keep in touch. Give it a little time. Work things out.

SANDY. When you see Ponyboy and Johnny explain to 'em. *(She touches his face.)* I sure love you.

SODAPOP *(a cry)*. Sandy—

(DARRY is coming back out, concerned about some-thing off L.)

DARRY. Looks like another fight over at the lot.
SANDY *(the trouble confirmed. Softly)*. Goodbye — *(She hurries off R.)*
SODAPOP *(after her)*. I'll write. You write back. *(But she's gone.)*
DARRY *(watching off L)*. Some Socs after Two-Bit. *(Re-laxing.)* Dallas's there.
SODAPOP *(bitterly)*. They sure got great timing.
DARRY *(considering SODAPOP)*. What about Sandy?
SODAPOP *(he doesn't want to talk about it)*. She has to visit her grandmother.
DARRY. You okay?
SODAPOP. Why not?

(TWO-BIT and DALLAS are coming on L.)

TWO-BIT *(cheerfully)*. Second time I been jumped this morning.
DALLAS. The Socs are a little tense this morning.
TWO-BIT *(what an understatement)*. Tense!
DARRY *(to DALLAS)*. I heard you told the fuzz Pony and Johnny were headed for Texas.
DALLAS *(vaguely)*. That would be one possibility.
DARRY. Could you think of another possibility? *(Sound of approaching car.)*
DALLAS *(he's not going to tell)*. You'd have to ask them.
TWO-BIT *(looking off)*. Man, look at the car. *(Admiring.)* Corvette Sting Ray.
DALLAS. Look at the redhead. *(Recognizing.)* The dead guy's girlfriend. Let's run that chick outa here.

TWO-BIT. Don't touch her, Dallas.

(CHERRY is coming on L, half in a trance.)

DALLAS. What's this? You're comin' on same as John-nycake.

CHERRY *(exhausted. Speaking with difficulty)*. How *is* Johnny?

DALLAS. We wouldn't know about that.

CHERRY. Would you know about Ponyboy?

DALLAS *(casually)*. The police think he may be headed southwest somewhere.

CHERRY *(worn out)*. It's necessary to jerk me around? *(As DALLAS shrugs, hitting back.)* At least we all know about Bob.

TWO-BIT *(quietly)*. Yeah.

DALLAS. Too bad about that.

CHERRY. Yeah. He's dead. Too bad.

DARRY. Would you wanta come in?

CHERRY. The reason I came over—the whole mess— maybe it's *my* fault.

DALLAS. So what about it?

CHERRY. Maybe I could help.

DALLAS *(incredulous)*. *You?*

TWO-BIT *(annoyed at DALLAS)*. Come on, Dallas—

DALLAS *(coming on to CHERRY)*. Maybe we could go over to the Dingo. I'll buy you a Coke—and we can talk about this 'n' that.

CHERRY *(it's too much)*. Pony and Johnny need some-one who can testify and you want to make out at the Dingo. *(She's going.)* Sorry—I have to get out of here.

DARRY. No, please—wait.

CHERRY. For what?

DARRY. It took a lot of nerve for you to come here this morning.

CHERRY. Yes, it did.

DALLAS. Any message for the juvenile delinquents?

CHERRY *(pause. Then with decision)*. Yes — tell them I said hi. *(She's off L. DALLAS starts to follow her.)*

DARRY. Dallas!

DALLAS *(looks back to DARRY)*. I only wanta talk to her. *(As DALLAS stares at him.)* Clear up about this testifying. *(Reasoning.)* Hey — don't worry.

DARRY. Talk nice, Dallas. You hear me?

DALLAS *(as he goes)*. I always talk nice.

SODAPOP *(puzzled by CHERRY's remark)*. Tell them I said hi? *(DARRY, SODAPOP and TWO-BIT are going off into the living area and the light is dimming off.)*

TWO-BIT. I heard they went to Texas.

DARRY *(to SODAPOP)*. Your kid brother's so smart — why can't he locate a telephone?

(Light comes up DR revealing PONYBOY, seated, leaning back against the old boards.)

PONYBOY. I'd been in church before. *(Looks about with apprehension.)* But this falling-down old place gave me a creepy feeling. What do you call it? Premonition? *(There's a long low whistle ending with a high note. Recognizing it with relief.)* That's our signal.

(JOHNNY hurries in with a sack of supplies.)

JOHNNY. Nobody paid any attention at the store. We're loaded up. *(He's starting to unpack.)* A week's supply of baloney, two loaves of bread, a box of matches, candy bars, candy bars —

PONYBOY. What else? More candy bars, and — *(He brings out a paperback book.)* Whee! *(Thrilled.)* Gone With the Wind! How'd you know I always wanted to read that book?

JOHNNY. I remember you sayin' something about it once. I thought maybe you could read it out loud and help kill time or something.

PONYBOY. Thanks. *(There's a pause as they BOTH consider.)*

JOHNNY. We're in big trouble.

PONYBOY. I'm still tired — and a little spooky. Things been happening so fast. Man, I'm tired.

JOHNNY. Last night. *(It's too much to remember.)* Was it last night?

PONYBOY *(nods)*. Last night we were walkin' Cherry and Marcia over to Two-Bit's. Last night we were layin' in the lot, lookin' up at the stars —

JOHNNY *(bitterly)*. Last night I killed that Bob. He couldn't of been over seventeen or eighteen, and I killed him. *(Leans back. Half a whisper.)* I'm real tired, too.

PONYBOY *(front)*. The next few days were the longest. We passed time playing poker and reading *Gone With the Wind.* Johnny was especially stuck on the Southern gentlemen.

JOHNNY. I bet they were cool ol' guys — ridin' into sure death because they were gallant. They remind me of Dallas.

PONYBOY. Dallas ain't got any more manners than I do. And you saw how he treated those girls at the Nightly Double.

JOHNNY. Yeah, but one night I saw Dallas gettin' picked up by the fuzz, and he kept real cool. They were gettin' him for somethin' Two-Bit did. And Dallas knew it. But he took the sentence without battin' an eye or even denying it. That's gallant.

PONYBOY. He's your hero now? Go back to sleep. *(JOHNNY sighs and leans back. PONYBOY continues, front.)* Dawn the next morning — all the lower valley was covered with mist. The clouds changed from gray to pink, and the mist was touched with gold. There was a silent moment when everything held its breath — then the sun rose.

JOHNNY. Golly — *(PONYBOY is startled by JOHNNY's voice.)* That's sure pretty.

PONYBOY. Wouldn't it be cool to be able to paint that sky? *(JOHNNY's standing to see, as is PONYBOY.)*

JOHNNY. Too bad it can't stay like that.

PONYBOY *(this triggers a memory for PONYBOY. He's quoting).* "Nothing gold can stay."

JOHNNY. What?

PONYBOY. A poem I read once. I was remembering it. *(As he recalls it.)*

> Nature's first green is gold
> Her hardest hue to hold
> Her early leaf's a flower;
> But only so an hour —

(Embarrassed.)

> It goes on.

JOHNNY *(wanting him to continue).* Well, you go on.

PONYBOY. Then leaf subsides to leaf

> So Eden sank to grief
> So dawn goes down to day

(He lets out a breath.)

Nothing gold can stay.

JOHNNY. Where'd you learn that?

PONYBOY. Robert Frost wrote it. *(Bothered.)* He meant more to it than I'm gettin' though.

JOHNNY. How come you remember it?

PONYBOY. Because I keep tryin' to figure it out. I never quite got what he meant by it.

JOHNNY. I never noticed colors and clouds and stuff till you started reminding me about them. It seems like they were never there before.

PONYBOY. I couldn't tell the others about stuff like that. I couldn't even remember the poem around them. They don't dig. Just you, and Sodapop sometimes — and maybe Cherry Valance.

JOHNNY *(with a pleased sigh)*. I guess we're different.

PONYBOY. Shoot, maybe *they* are. *(Front again.)* I was so tired of baloney, I got sick lookin' at it. We'd eaten all the candy bars, and I was dying for a Pepsi. By that time, I'd read up to Sherman's siege of Atlanta, and I owed Johnny a hundred and fifty bucks from poker games. *(Amused at himself.)* I was beginning to think I'd always lived in a church, or maybe during the Civil War — or both. *(There's a low whistle signal ending with the sudden high note.)*

JOHNNY. Pony — hear it? *(The whistle is repeated.)*

PONYBOY *(tense)*. Who d'ya think?

(DALLAS is crossing to them.)

DALLAS. Glory — look at the church mice.

JOHNNY. Hey, Dallas!

DALLAS. Little Johnnycake and — Ponyboy.

PONYBOY *(smiling)*. Never thought I'd be so glad to see Dallas Winston.

JOHNNY. What's happening?

PONYBOY. How's Sodapop? Are the fuzz after us? Is Darry all right? Do the boys know where we are?

DALLAS. Hold it. I can't answer everything at once. You want to eat first? I skipped breakfast and I'm about starving.

JOHNNY *(indignant)*. *You're* starving?

PONYBOY. If you'd like some baloney—

DALLAS. No thanks. The fuzz won't be lookin' for you around here. They think you lit out the other direction. I got Buck's T-bird parked down the road. *(Looks at them.)* Ain't you been eatin' anything?

JOHNNY. What gives you that idea?

DALLAS. You both look terrible. The cops think you're in Texas.

PONYBOY. Why Texas?

DALLAS. They know me. I get hauled in for everything that happens on our turf. I let drop you were headed somewhere else. *(Wicked smile.)* They beat it outa me.

JOHNNY *(to PONYBOY)*. Like I told ya—gallant.

DALLAS. Do y'all want somethin' to eat or not?

PONYBOY. Believe it!

JOHNNY. Be good to get in a car again. *(DALLAS and JOHNNY are facing front as though sitting in the front seat of a car. PONYBOY stands just to the side of them.)*

PONYBOY. Dallas always did like to drive fast as if he didn't care whether he got where he was goin' or not. We came down the red dirt road so fast Johnny and I got a little green. Then we stopped at a Dairy Queen.

(There's a wood table and a bench on L now with fast food on it. JOHNNY and DALLAS are seated first. As PONYBOY comes up to the table, he takes a Pepsi off of it.)

PONYBOY *(with satisfaction).* First thing I got was a Pepsi. Then we started gorging. *(He joins them.)*

JOHNNY. I'm gonna start next on banana splits — *(Bad thoughts are coming back to PONYBOY, and he pushes the food in front of him away.)*

PONYBOY. I guess it's time you tell us what's goin' on. *(They ALL get serious.)*

DALLAS *(leans forward. Strong low voice).* The Socs and us are having all-out warfare all over the city. That kid you killed had plenty of friends and all over town it's Soc against grease. We can't walk alone at all. I started carrying a heater.

PONYBOY. Dallas! You kill people with heaters!

DALLAS. Ya kill 'em with switchblades, too, don't ya, kid?

JOHNNY *(miserable).* Please, Dallas —

PONYBOY *(worried).* If you walk around with a gun —

DALLAS. Don't worry. My heater ain't loaded. I ain't aimin' to get picked up for murder — *(Cheerfully.)* But it sure does help a bluff.

PONYBOY. All-out warfare all over the city?

DALLAS. Just one more day. *(Deciding to tell them.)* We're having it out. Once and for all. Us and the Socs. Tomorrow night. The vacant lot.

JOHNNY. Tomorrow night!

DALLAS. You guys'll miss it. *(Leaning forward.)* We got hold of the president of their social club and had a war council. So here's the deal. No weapons. If we run —

things go on as usual. If they run — they stay outa our territory, but good! Out! *(Determined.)* I don't care how many Socs show up — they're gonna run.

JOHNNY. Suppose they bring chains?

DALLAS. Hey, I didn't tell you. We got us a spy. *(As they BOTH look at him.)* That good-lookin' broad I tried to pick up that night you killed the Soc. The redhead. Cherry what's-her-name.

PONYBOY and JOHNNY *(together)*. Cherry!

JOHNNY. The Soc?

DALLAS. Man, next time I want a broad, I'll pick up my own kind.

PONYBOY. We were gettin' that same advice from the Socs.

DALLAS *(incredulous)*. Cherry the Soc helpin' us!

PONYBOY *(defensively)*. She isn't Cherry the Soc. She's —

DALLAS *(not getting this)*. Anyway — she said if Johnny comes to trial she'll testify that the Socs were drunk and looking for a fight — and you only fought back in self-defense. How about that?

JOHNNY. That would really help.

DALLAS *(a grim laugh)*. Then I suggested we go for a ride in Buck's T-bird. She said, "No, thank you." Then very polite — she told me where to go. *(Indignant.)* What'd I do wrong?

PONYBOY. Maybe you shoulda tried a little conversation before makin' your move.

DALLAS *(that's stupid)*. Conversation! *(Looking about.)* This place is out of it. What do they do for kicks in the country, play checkers?

JOHNNY *(has been deciding)*. We're goin' back and turn ourselves in.

DALLAS *(looks at JOHNNY, then at the sky, then back at JOHNNY)*. What?

JOHNNY. We're goin' back an' turn ourselves in. I got a good chance of bein' let off easy. I ain't got no record. Both Ponyboy and Cherry can testify it was self-defense.

DALLAS. Once they get their hands on you —

JOHNNY. I can't stay in that church the rest of my life.

DALLAS. When they take you in you'll find out — greasers get it worse than anyone.

JOHNNY. We won't tell that you helped us, and we'll give you what's left of the money —

DALLAS. You sure you want to go back?

JOHNNY *(nods)*. It ain't fair for Ponyboy to have to stay up in the church with Darry and Soda worrying about him all the time —

PONYBOY. Darry don't —

JOHNNY. Yes, he does. *(To DALLAS.)* I don't guess — *(Swallows, trying not to look eager.)* I don't guess my parents are worried about me or anything?

DALLAS *(matter-of-fact voice)*. The boys are worried. Two-Bit was for going to Texas to look for you.

JOHNNY *(doggedly)*. My parents, did *they* ask about me?

DALLAS. No, they didn't. *(In pain for his friend.)* Johnny, what do they matter? *(Passionately.)* Shoot, my old man don't give a hang whether I'm in jail, or dead in a car wreck or drunk in the gutter. *(Trying to make JOHNNY believe it.)* That don't bother me none.

PONYBOY. Let's go back to the church. I left a book there. *(They're leaving the table.)*

DALLAS. Get in the car. *(Growling to JOHNNY.)* If you'd turned yourself in five days ago, it'd saved a lot of trouble. C'mon.

JOHNNY *(as they start R)*. I was scared. I still am. *(The THREE of them are lined up as though in the front seat of a car with DALLAS driving.)*

DALLAS. I ain't mad at you, Johnny. I just don't want you to get hurt. You don't know what a few months in jail can do to you.

JOHNNY *(touched. Realizing)*. Like it happened to you. *(Off R there's a red glow.)*

DALLAS *(concentrating on the driving)*. You get mean. *(Sounds of PEOPLE calling to each other in the distance.)*

PONYBOY. We got to the top of the hill, and Dallas slammed on the brakes. We couldn't believe what was happening.

DALLAS *(staring off)*. Glory — the church is on fire.

PONYBOY *(apparently getting out of the car)*. Let's go.

DALLAS *(irritated)*. What for? Get back in the car.

JOHNNY. People over there —

DALLAS. It's not our problem.

(JOHNNY and PONYBOY are going R, as a man, JERRY, enters with some young CHILDREN, if available.)

DALLAS. If you don't get back in the car — *(But they're going. DALLAS's furious but he follows them.)*

PONYBOY *(to JERRY)*. What's going on? *(Sounds of a fire are beginning.)*

JERRY. We don't know. We're having a school outing, and suddenly the place is burning. Kids with matches!

PONYBOY *(to JOHNNY)*. Our matches. *(The roar and crackling is getting louder and the red is more intense.)*

JERRY *(calling)*. Stand back, children. Wait for the fire-men.

(MRS. O'BRIANT rushes in.)

MRS. O'BRIANT *(to JERRY)*. Some of the kids are missing.

JERRY. They're 'round somewhere.

MRS. O'BRIANT. They're missing. They were — *(She holds up her hand for quiet. There's the cry of several terrified CHILDREN heard just above the sound of the fire.)* They're *in the church!*

JOHNNY. We'll get them. Don't worry.

JERRY. No. Wait for the firemen.

JOHNNY. There ain't time. *(JOHNNY rushes off R. Sound of the fire increases. CHILDREN, if available, are crying in fear.)*

MRS. O'BRIANT *(a prayer)*. God, help us. *(MRS. O'BRIANT and JERRY exit in the direction of the fire.)*

PONYBOY. What I remember — we slammed a big rock through the window and pulled ourselves in. *(As he goes.)* Hey, Johnny!

PONYBOY'S VOICE *(shouting)*. Hand me that kid, Johnny.

JOHNNY'S VOICE. Hey — got a little one! Out the window little guy!

PONYBOY'S VOICE. You enjoying this, Johnnycake? There's another back in the smoke.

DALLAS *(shouting off into the red glow and roar of the fire)*. Get *outa* there! Get out! The roof's gonna cave in. *(Screaming.)* Forget the stupid kids!

PONYBOY *(off)*. Here's the last one! *(The sound of the fire is climaxing. PONYBOY shouts.)* Roof is going!

(There's the sound of an awful crash and a terrible cry from JOHNNY.)

(PONYBOY staggers on and DALLAS throws him down and is clubbing his back. Except for fire, the light is dimming fast. The stage is black. In the darkness there's the siren of an ambulance and, if available, the light effect of a twirling red warning beacon thrown against the back of the stage. There's also the sound of a vehicle being driven fast. Light comes up DC revealing PONYBOY, laid out on a stretcher, if possible one that's raised up and on wheels. The man from the church fire, JERRY, is sitting beside PONYBOY, and the woman from that event, MRS. O'BRIANT, is holding onto the side of the stretcher and gently sponging PONYBOY's face.)

MRS. O'BRIANT. I think he's coming around.

JERRY. Thank you, Mrs. O'Briant.

PONYBOY *(trying to sit up and see)*. Where ya takin' me?

JERRY. Lie back, kid. You're in an ambulance.

PONYBOY *(frightened)*. Ambulance? *(A cry.)* Where's Johnny? Where's Dallas?

JERRY. They're in the ambulance right behind us.

MRS. O'BRIANT. Just calm down. You're going to be okay. You just passed out.

PONYBOY. I didn't pass out. Dallas hit me. He knocked me out.

JERRY. Because your back was in flames.

PONYBOY *(surprised)*. It was? I didn't feel it.

JERRY. Your friend put it out before you got burned.

PONYBOY *(grimly)*. Are you takin' us to the police station?

MRS. O'BRIANT *(startled)*. The *police* station?

JERRY. Why would we take you to the police station? We're taking all of you to the hospital.

PONYBOY *(digests this for an instant)*. Johnny and Dallas are all right?

JERRY *(hesitating)*. Which one's which?

PONYBOY. Johnny has black hair. Dallas's the mean-looking one.

JERRY *(speaking carefully)*. Dallas will be all right. He burned one arm trying to drag the other kid out the window. Johnny— *(He takes a breath.)* I don't know about Johnny. A piece of timber caught him across the back—he might have a broken back.

MRS. O'BRIANT. He has severe burns. Severe. *(PONY-BOY has sat up at this, horrified.)* They're giving him plasma now.

JERRY. Better lie back. It's better if you— *(Overwhelmed by it all.)* I swear, you three are the bravest kids I've ever seen. *(Trying to put it lightly.)* Are you professional heroes or something?

MRS. O'BRIANT *(deeply moved)*. I think you were sent straight from Heaven.

PONYBOY. Are the little kids okay?

MRS. O'BRIANT. They're okay—thank you. *(The light is dimming off on them.)* A lot of parents want to thank you. *(As the light, the red flasher and the vehicle sounds fade off, a VOICE is heard calling over the hospital public address.)*

VOICE. Doctor Morse. Report to emergency. Doctor Morse. Report to emergency.

(Light is coming up. PONYBOY is standing at the left, and as he speaks a DOCTOR and a NURSE cross in front of him and go off.)

PONYBOY. They checked me over and except for a few burns and a big bruise across my back, I was all right.

(A HOSPITAL WORKER is wheeling in a stretcher with DALLAS on it.)

PONYBOY. Hey, Dallas...

DALLAS *(trying to grin. Trying to sit up)*. If you ever do a stupid thing like that again, I'll beat the tar out of you. *(He's being wheeled off.)* You hear me? Don't you ever!

PONYBOY *(after him)*. Dallas, listen —

(PONYBOY looks back as another stretcher is coming on. This one has JOHNNY who is pale, eyes closed and motionless.)

PONYBOY *(softly)*. Johnny — *(There is no response. Calling after JOHNNY as he is wheeled off.)* Johnnycake —

(JERRY is coming in R, crossing to PONYBOY.)

JERRY. Mrs. O'Briant was just talking to some reporters. *(Glancing left, then back to PONYBOY.)* And some people phoned from the front reception. They're on their way up. Claim to be your brothers or something.

PONYBOY *(excited)*. My brothers?

JERRY *(smiles)*. That's what they said.

PONYBOY. But — how'd they know?

JERRY *(going off R)*. Phone number in your wallet.

(SODAPOP races on L. Stops as he sees PONYBOY.)

SODAPOP *(can hardly believe it)*. Pony!

PONYBOY *(overjoyed)*. Sodapop! *(SODAPOP grabs PONY-BOY in a bear hug and swings him back and forth.)*

SODAPOP *(as he swings PONYBOY)*. Where you been? How come you didn't call? You tryin' to scare us to death?

(As this is happening, DARRY comes on L. He's a little hesitant. After all, the last time he saw PONYBOY he slapped him. As SODAPOP and PONYBOY finish their affectionate pummeling of each other, DARRY calls.)

DARRY *(half pleading)*. Ponyboy. *(PONYBOY turns and sees him. They look at each other for a moment. Then PONYBOY shouts and rushes to DARRY.)*

PONYBOY. DARRY! *(They grab each other and hug.)* Darry, I'm sorry! I shoulda—I meant to—

DARRY *(full of emotion)*. I thought we'd lost you—like we did Mom and Dad. *(As ALL THREE BROTHERS are laughing and hugging.)*

SODAPOP. Don't look like you got much sleep this week.

PONYBOY. Hardly slept at all.

SODAPOP. Neither did we.

(The DOCTOR is coming back on with the NURSE.)

DARRY *(calling)*. Doctor—we're taking our kid brother home.

DOCTOR. He'll be fine. There's no paperwork. You can go along home.

DARRY. I asked about Johnny and Dallas, but no one would tell us anything.

NURSE. Are you members of the family?

DOCTOR. I'll only talk to the families.

DARRY *(quietly firm)*. Doctor—Johnny and Dallas don't have any family 'cept us.

SODAPOP *(agreeing)*. I think we're about as much family as they have.

DOCTOR *(deciding)*. All right. *(To the GROUP.)* Dallas Winston should be okay after two or three days in the hospital. One arm is pretty bad, but he'll get back the use of it.

PONYBOY *(he thought so)*. Dallas is always okay.

DARRY *(wanting to hear the worst)*. Tell us about Johnny.

NURSE *(to DOCTOR)*. We already phoned his parents.

DARRY *(controlling his emotions)*. Tell it to us straight.

DOCTOR. Johnny Cade is critical. His back is broken. He's in severe shock and suffering from third-degree burns. *(The THREE BROTHERS are in shock.)*

DARRY *(keeping his voice controlled)*. What are you doing for him?

DOCTOR. Everything to ease the pain, but because his back is broken, he can't feel the burns below the waist. Even if he lives—

PONYBOY *(stung)*. If? You said *if?*

DOCTOR. If he lives, he'll be a cripple.

DARRY. Is he conscious?

DOCTOR. In and out.

NURSE. He keeps calling for Dallas and Ponyboy.

DARRY. Can we see him?

DOCTOR. Not now. What you do now is you go home and you get some rest.

PONYBOY *(he can't deal with it)*. If he lives—

VOICE *(on P.A.)*. Doctor Morse, pick up line four, please.

DOCTOR. You wanted it straight. You got it straight.

DARRY *(level)*. That's right, Doctor.

VOICE *(on P.A.)*. Doctor Morse, pick up line four, please.

DOCTOR *(he has to go)*. You can phone in later and check with the Nurse's station on this floor. *(The DOCTOR and the NURSE are going off L.)*

DARRY *(rubs the back of PONYBOY's head)*. We'd better go home. We can't do anything here. *(They're walking into the living area which is now the focus of the light. PONYBOY pauses outside as his BROTHERS go in and then exit.)*

PONYBOY. A pain was growing in my throat. The doctor gave it to us straight, all right. I tried to think—maybe I'm dreaming. Maybe I'll wake up at home and everything'll be like it used to be—only it was getting harder and harder to lie to myself.

(Light is coming up. TWO-BIT is coming on carrying some newspapers.)

PONYBOY. Next morning Two-Bit came over same as usual, only earlier.

TWO-BIT. You can't believe a thing they put in the papers anymore. Who'd believe two greasy lookin' mugs could be heroes. *(Incredible.)* How do you like bein' a hero, big shot?

PONYBOY. How do I like *what?*

TWO-BIT *(shoving paper in front of him)*. Like a big shot — *(Reading.)* "Juvenile Delinquents Turn Heroes." *(Smiling.)* I like that "Turn" bit.

PONYBOY. I guess we turned all of a sudden.

TWO-BIT. It says you and Johnny risked your lives. One of the parents said the little kids would've burned to death if it hadn't been for the two of you. Tells about the fight, too. *You* have to appear in juvenile court for running away, and *Johnny* — for manslaughter — *(Reading.)* if he recovers.

PONYBOY. Why do they keep saying *if?*

TWO-BIT. They go on about how Darry 'n' Soda are working so you can all stay together, and you been on the honor roll at school. *(Adding.)* The reporter puts in the three of you shouldn't be separated after working so hard to stay together.

PONYBOY. Separated?

TWO-BIT. Won't happen. The juvenile court don't do things like that to heroes. *(Suddenly serious.)* I was thinkin' of lookin' in on Johnnycake. *(He needs help.)* Wanna come with me?

(MARCIA is coming on.)

PONYBOY. It's a little early. I don't know about visiting hours.

TWO-BIT *(worried)*. I can't wait for visiting hours.

MARCIA *(calls)*. Ponyboy —

TWO-BIT. Look who's —

MARCIA *(soberly)*. Hello, Two-Bit.

TWO-BIT. I know. You want a lift home in my car.

MARCIA *(pleasantly)*. No thanks. I'm with someone. He wants to talk to Pony.

PONYBOY. Who is it?

MARCIA. Randy Anderson.

PONYBOY *(startled)*. Why should I talk to Randy? He's a Soc. It's their fault Bob's dead. It's their fault Johnny's in the hospital. It's their fault Soda and I might get put in a boys' home.

MARCIA. I know that. Randy knows that.

(RANDY is coming on R where he stops and watches.)

MARCIA *(nods toward RANDY. To PONYBOY)*. Up to you. I have to go.

TWO-BIT. Can I give you a lift?

MARCIA. Maybe sometime. *(MARCIA is gone.)*

RANDY *(calls to PONYBOY)*. Can we talk?

TWO-BIT *(to RANDY)*. You know the rules. No jazz before the rumble.

RANDY. I know the rules. *(PONYBOY looks at TWO-BIT who shrugs.)*

TWO-BIT. Meet me at the car pretty quick. We have to see Johnny. *(TWO-BIT goes L as PONYBOY turns back to look at RANDY.)*

RANDY. I read about you in the paper. How come?

PONYBOY. Maybe I felt like playing hero.

RANDY *(bothered)*. I wouldn't have done it. I'd a let those kids burn to death.

PONYBOY. You might not have. You might have done the same thing.

RANDY. I can't believe a greaser could pull something like that.

PONYBOY *(sharp)*. Greaser didn't have anything to do with it! Two-Bit wouldn't've done it. Maybe you would. It's the individual.

RANDY. Maybe you're right. *(Takes a breath.)* I'm not going to show at the rumble tonight. *(PONYBOY is surprised.)* I'm sick of all this. And no matter what you think, Bob was a good guy. He had a problem, but he was a real person.

PONYBOY. How could I know that?

RANDY. You couldn't, and now he's dead. His mother had a total breakdown.

PONYBOY. Who's to blame?

RANDY. All I know, they spoiled him; they gave in to him all the time. He kept trying to make someone say "No" and they never did. He needed somebody to lay down the law, set limits, give him something to stand on. *(Tries to grin, but he's close to tears.)* One time he came home drunker than anything—falling down disgusting. He thought sure they'd raise the roof. *(It's so absurd.)* Know what they did? They said it was *their* fault, they'd failed him, *they* took the blame. Maybe if his father had given him a belt instead, he'd still be alive. *(With a small smile.)* Only person ever told Bob "No" was Cherry Valance. No wonder he was so crazy about her.

PONYBOY. I have to go to the hospital.

RANDY. That kid—your buddy—he might die?

PONYBOY. He might.

RANDY. And tonight—people get hurt in rumbles, maybe killed. And it doesn't do any good. Even if you whip us, you'll still be at the bottom and we'll still be the lucky ones with all the breaks. Greasers will still be greasers, and Socs will still be Socs. I'm going to get out of this town.

PONYBOY. Running away won't help.

RANDY *(in a bind)*. I'm marked chicken if I punk out at the rumble, and I'd hate myself if I didn't. So what can I do?

PONYBOY. I'd help if I could.

RANDY. No you wouldn't. I'm a Soc. You get a little money and the whole world hates you.

PONYBOY. No, you hate the whole world.

(TWO-BIT is coming on.)

PONYBOY. I have to go. *(Pauses.)* You'd have saved those kids, same as we did.

RANDY. Thanks, grease. *(He stops.)* I didn't mean that. I meant, thanks, kid.

PONYBOY. My name's Ponyboy. *(He's headed for TWO-BIT.)* Nice talkin' to you, Randy. *(RANDY gives a brief wave, then hurries off.)*

TWO-BIT. What'd Mr. Super Soc have to say?

PONYBOY *(briefly)*. He ain't a Soc. He's just a guy. He just wanted to talk. *(Hospital sounds.)*

(The NURSE comes on, crossing to them.)

NURSE. You shouldn't even be up on this floor. Your friend's in critical condition. No visitors. Absolutely.

TWO-BIT. It's my buddy in there — Hey, lady — *please!*

(The DOCTOR is also coming on.)

PONYBOY *(hopefully)*. Might be good for him to see us.

DOCTOR. Let them go in, Nurse. *(To the BOYS.)* He's been asking for you. *(Back to the NURSE.)* It can't hurt now.

NURSE. He's over here. *(She's leading them to the side where there's a screen set up.)*

PONYBOY *(digesting this. Uneasily)*. It can't hurt now?

(The NURSE is folding back the screen revealing JOHNNY on a white cot, if possible with some accompanying hospital paraphernalia.)

TWO-BIT *(startled by what he sees, but trying to be cheerful)*. Hey, Johnnycake. Johnnycake —

JOHNNY *(slowly opening his eyes and managing a smile)*. Hey, y'all.

TWO-BIT *(eager to make him smile. This is TWO-BIT's way)*. Got a riddle for ya — What's the safest thing to be when you meet a gang of social outcasts in an alley?

JOHNNY *(unable)*. Dunno —

PONYBOY *(having to go with it)*. A judo expert?

TWO-BIT. No. Another social outcast! *(TWO-BIT yelps at his wit, and JOHNNY tries to smile along.)* They treatin' you okay? *(JOHNNY nods.)* Listen. *(Glances about. Confiding.)* We're having the big rumble tonight. *(JOHNNY registers on this but doesn't say anything.)* Too bad you 'n' Dallas can't be in it. We're gonna get 'em off our backs! Get 'em off our territory for good! *(JOHNNY nods with an effort.)*

PONYBOY. You got your name in the paper for being a hero! Yeah, *you.*

JOHNNY *(almost grins)*. Tuff!

PONYBOY *(encouraging him)*. I figure Southern gentlemen got nothing on Johnny Cade!

JOHNNY *(remembering)*. The book that got burned — can you get another one?

TWO-BIT. What book, Johnny?

PONYBOY. He wants a copy of *Gone With the Wind* so I can finish readin' it to him.

TWO-BIT *(volunteering)*. I'll go down to the drugstore 'n' get him one. It's just downstairs. *(As he goes.)* Don't y'all run away. *(PONYBOY pulls a chair up beside JOHNNY.)*

PONYBOY. Dallas's gonna be all right. And Darry and me—we're okay now. *(JOHNNY has closed his eyes.)* Johnny?

JOHNNY. It just hurts sometimes. It usually don't—I can't feel anything below the middle of my back. *(He breaths hard for a moment.)* I'm pretty bad off, ain't I, Pony?

PONYBOY. You'll be okay. You gotta be. We couldn't get along without you.

(DALLAS, wearing a white hospital robe, has come in and stands just inside, not yet seen by the OTHERS.)

JOHNNY. I won't be able to walk again.

PONYBOY *(keeping hold of himself with an effort)*. You'll be okay. I'm tellin' you—

JOHNNY. I'm so scared. I used to talk about killing my-self, but I don't want to die. *(With what strength he has.)* It ain't long enough, Ponyboy. Sixteen years ain't long enough. There's so much stuff I ain't done yet, and so many things I ain't seen. That time we were at the church in Windrixville was the only time I've been away from our neighborhood.

PONYBOY. You ain't gonna die.

DALLAS. That's right, Johnny.

JOHNNY. Dallas?

DALLAS. Still here, Johnnycake. *(Trying to interest him.)* Your picture's in the paper. Mine, too. Some guys came by to rub it in about me missing the rumble tonight. Said when they saw my picture they couldn't believe it didn't have "Wanted Dead or Alive" under it.

JOHNNY. That's a good one, Dallas.

DALLAS. We're gonna win that fight tonight.

(The NURSE enters.)

DALLAS. We're gonna clean out our neighborhood good.

NURSE *(quietly)*. Johnny. Your mother's here to see you.

JOHNNY *(agitated)*. She—I don't want to see her.

NURSE. She's your mother.

JOHNNY. She's come to tell me about all the trouble I'm causing her. Well tell her to leave me alone. For once. For once just leave me alone. *(JOHNNY falls back on the pillow exhausted and breathing hard.)*

NURSE. I was afraid of something like this. You'll have to go. Please.

(TWO-BIT is rushing on with a paperback book.)

DALLAS. Be back later, Johnny.

TWO-BIT. The book—

NURSE *(takes it)*. I'll give it to him. *(Wanting them to leave.)* We need the doctor. Please—

DALLAS *(as he goes)*. We're gonna stomp 'em tonight, Johnny. *(TWO- BIT is going off L. PONYBOY, with too much on his mind, is coming DC.)*

NURSE *(pauses by the bed)*. They brought a book for you, Johnny. *(Reading title.)* Gone With the Wind.

(JOHNNY is calming down.) We can read it together a little later. *(She hands him the book.)*

JOHNNY *(as he looks at book)*. Could I have a piece of paper and a pencil?

NURSE *(nodding)*. When I come back. *(JOHNNY is happy to be holding the book. As the NURSE turns to go off R, she sees SOMEONE. NURSE is calling off.)* I'm sorry, but you can't come in.

VOICE *(JOHNNY's mother)*. I'm *supposed* to see him. He's my son.

NURSE. Please, not now.

VOICE. This is our thanks – after all the trouble we've gone to raising him. He'd rather be with hoodlums! *(JOHNNY sinks back onto the bed.)*

NURSE *(off.)* The doctor will talk to you later.

(The DOCTOR comes on R to look at JOHNNY, followed by the NURSE who is re-setting the screen in front of JOHNNY. CHERRY comes on L, standing just inside. As PONYBOY turns to go, he sees her.)

CHERRY *(gives him a nervous smile)*. Thought I'd find you here.

PONYBOY. Hi, Cherry. *(Uncomfortable. Starting to go.)* Nice to see you –

CHERRY. Ponyboy, stay a minute.

PONYBOY. Sure. *(Looking for something to say.)* It's gonna be rough tonight.

CHERRY. Randy's not going to show up for the rumble.

PONYBOY. I know.

CHERRY. He's not scared. He's just sick of fighting. Bob was his best friend. Since grade school.

PONYBOY *(with an edge)*. Johnnycake ain't showin' up either. Only I can't say he ain't scared. He's real scared.

CHERRY *(abashed)*. How bad is Johnny?

PONYBOY. Bad. You can't see him just now, but, please, will you go up sometime?

CHERRY *(with difficulty)*. No. I couldn't.

PONYBOY. Why not?

CHERRY *(a quiet, desperate voice)*. Because he killed Bob. I know — Bob asked for it. He made it happen — but I couldn't look at the person who killed him.

PONYBOY. I don't get it.

CHERRY. You only know his bad side. When he got drunk he was horrible — it's that part of him that beat up Johnny. I knew it was Bob when you told me the story. *(Bitterly.)* He was so proud of those rings. *(Trying to sort it out.)* When he wasn't trying to destroy himself, he could be something special — something that marked him different.

PONYBOY. Last time I saw Bob he was drowning me.

CHERRY *(bitterly)*. Think hard, Ponyboy. When was the last time you saw, Bob?

PONYBOY *(as he remembers)*. Last time I saw him he was —

CHERRY *(as PONYBOY winces)*. Don't go to the rumble tonight.

PONYBOY. They bringin' blades?

CHERRY. No. They play your way. No weapons. Fair deal. Your rules. Randy told me. He knows for sure. I already told Darry.

PONYBOY. I guess we're supposed to be grateful.

CHERRY. I'm not looking for gratitude. I only want to help. I like you, Ponyboy. I liked you from the start —

the way you talk. Wouldn't you try to help me if you could?

PONYBOY. Sure — if I could.

CHERRY. I have to testify at your hearing. Randy, too.

PONYBOY. To clear Bob's good name?

CHERRY. You'll be there. You'll find out. *(As she looks at him.)* You'd make a good friend, Pony. Good friends are a little hard to find these days.

PONYBOY. I have to go.

CHERRY *(disappointed)*. Sure.

PONYBOY. Hey — *(Suddenly he smiles.)* Can you see the sunset real good from your side of town?

CHERRY *(startled. Smiling back)*. Real good.

PONYBOY. You can see it good from our side, too.

CHERRY. Thanks, Ponyboy. *(Smiling back at him.)* You dig okay.

(As she goes out, light comes up in the living area. TWO-BIT is coming up to PONYBOY.)

TWO-BIT. Wondered what happened to you. *(Concerned.)* You feel okay? You look awful.

PONYBOY. I got a headache, but don't tell Darry, okay? I'll take a bunch of aspirins.

TWO-BIT. If you're really sick, and go ahead and fight anyway —

PONYBOY. Keep your mouth shut. Darry won't know a thing.

TWO-BIT. You'd think you could get away with murder living with your big brother, but Darry's stricter with you than your folks. *(They're going into living area.)*

PONYBOY. Yeah, but they raised two boys before me. Darry hasn't. *(TWO-BIT is joining SODAPOP and DARRY inside, helping himself to more hair oil.)*

DARRY *(glances at PONYBOY)*. You don't look so great, kid. You're tensed up.

SODAPOP. We all get tensed up before a rumble.

TWO-BIT. Skin never hurt anyone. No weapons; no danger.

DARRY *(looking closer)*. You got a fever?

PONYBOY. I'll be okay. I'll get hold of a little one.

DARRY. If you get in a jam, holler.

PONYBOY. Promise.

TWO-BIT. It's getting to be that time. Is everybody happy? *(Note: In the original, they accompanied the following words with gymnastics. Unless the ACTORS doing these roles are especially qualified, they should simply horse around.)*

SODAPOP *(chanting)*. I am a greaser. I am a JD and a hood. I blacken the name of our fair city.

TWO-BIT *(in a snobbish voice)*. Get thee hence, white trash. I am a Soc. I am the privileged and the well dressed. I throw beer blasts, drive fancy cars, break windows at fancy parties.

PONYBOY. And what do you do for fun?

ALL *(together. Shouting)*. We jump greasers! *(The lights go out in the living area behind them and the stage is almost dark. Suddenly they stand together quietly and waiting.)*

TWO-BIT. Where's Tim and the others?

DARRY. They'll be here. *(Noticing.)* They're coming.

(GREASER EXTRAS are moving in quietly to stand with those already there. Sound of cars approaching.)

SODAPOP. That's not all that's coming.

(The sound of cars stopping, doors being slammed. A group of SOC EXTRAS are coming on in a group that spreads out across the left side of the stage. They are, of course, much better dressed than the GREASERS. The TWO LINES are facing each other. This is taking place in semi-darkness, broken by someone on each side with a flashlight. A SOC steps forward.)

SOC *(shouting)*. Let's get the rules straight—nothing but fists, and the first to run lose. Right?

TWO-BIT *(shouts back)*. You savvy real good. *(There's an uneasy silence. Then DARRY steps forward.)*

DARRY. I'll take on anyone. *(A drum starts to beat slowly. A husky SOC steps forward to face DARRY. His name is PAUL.)*

PAUL *(quietly)*. Hello, Darrel.

DARRY. Hello, Paul. *(A drum with a different sound begins slowly from the other side as PAUL and DARRY face each other. A dim spot has come up on PONYBOY who is standing front and to the side. SODAPOP comes next to PONYBOY.)*

SODAPOP *(aside to PONYBOY)*. Paul Holden. He was the best back on Darry's football team at high school.

PONYBOY. That Soc?

SODAPOP. They used to buddy around. He's gotta be a junior in college by now.

PONYBOY. And Darry's gotta work.

PAUL *(to DARRY)*. I'll take you. *(The drums-in-conflict pick up a little.)*

DARRY *(quietly)*. You think you can handle me, Paul?

PAUL *(with contempt).* I can handle any greaser. *(The GROUP is stirring in place as DARRY and PAUL start to circle each other.)*

PONYBOY *(tense).* Made me think of a book by Jack London—where the wolf pack waits for one of two members to go down in a fight. But it's different here. The moment either one swings—the rumble is on. *(DALLAS shouting is rushing into the action.)*

DALLAS. Hold up! Wait for me!

DARRY *(looks over to him. Shouting).* Dallas? *(At this, PAUL throws a sneak punch, which DARRY manages to block. There's a roar from both sides as the TWO GROUPS go at each other in the dark. No light except for the spot isolating PONYBOY and the TWO waving flashlights. Both drums are pounding and there are shouts and cries.)*

PONYBOY. I couldn't find a little Soc so I grabbed the next size up. Dallas was fighting a big one next to me. *(He yells at DALLAS.)* Dallas—I thought you were in the hospital.

DALLAS *(voice from darkness).* I was! I ain't now. *(The action swirls in the darkness.)*

PONYBOY. I wanted to ask Dallas how he got out, but a Soc—who was heavier than I took him for—was slugging the sense out of me. I thought he was going to knock out my teeth. By the time Darry got through with him—Paul was crawling out on his hands and knees. Darry saw what was happening to me and he lifted the big guy off me and knocked him back three feet. I figured I should help Dallas since he could only use one arm. *(Drums and shouts are reaching a climax.)* I jumped on the back of the Soc that was slugging Dallas, but he threw me over his shoulder. Someone kicked me in the ribs, and you better believe it hurt. Dallas grabbed him, but this time he kicked me so hard in the head I was stunned. *(He looks over at the action.)* I'm lying there stunned — then all of a sudden, greasers start shouting. *(The drums stop. Joyful VOICES. The SOCS are disappearing off L, pursued by GREASER EXTRAS.)*

VOICES *(exultant)*. They're *running!* The Socs are *running!* We stomped 'em! *Look at 'em run! (Several GREASERS are doing a victory dance.)*

DARRY *(shouts)*. Keep after them! Chase 'em home!

TWO-BIT. Chase 'em to Mexico! *(DARRY is coming up to PONYBOY.)*

DARRY. You okay, kid?

PONYBOY *(wryly)*. I'll let you know after I count my teeth.

DARRY. We got some guys hurt. *(Starting to go.)* I better check 'em out. *(Some remaining GREASERS are going off, shouting about their victory. DARRY is checking PEOPLE out as he goes. It's getting quiet. Out of the darkness DALLAS, now beat, comes over to PONYBOY.)*

DALLAS *(urgent)*. Pony — come on! We have to go.

PONYBOY. Where?

DALLAS. To see Johnny! We have to tell Johnny!

PONYBOY. Right now?

DALLAS. Right now. He was gettin' worse when I left. He asked to see you. *(Gestures.)* I got a car over here.

PONYBOY *(catching the urgency)*. Hey, let's go!

(They BOTH turn from where they're standing to look over to the hospital area where light is coming up reveal-

ing the DOCTOR bending over JOHNNY with the
NURSE beside him.)

PONYBOY. We got there in nothing flat. *(As they start*
toward JOHNNY, the DOCTOR comes a few steps to
meet them.)

DOCTOR *(holding up a hand)*. Wait right there, boys.
You can't see him. He's dying.

PONYBOY *(softly)*. *Dying.*

DALLAS *(his voice shaken)*. We gotta see him. *(He brings*
out a revolver. He's a little unsteady on his feet.) We're
gonna see Johnny, and if you give me any static you'll
end up on your own operating table!

PONYBOY *(to the DOCTOR)*. He asked for us. *(Plead-*
ing.) We're his family.

NURSE *(to DOCTOR)*. Shall I call security?

DOCTOR *(to DALLAS and PONYBOY)*. You can see
him, but it's because you're his friends – his family, not
because of the gun. *(To NURSE.)* Yes, call security.
(DALLAS looks at him for a moment and puts the re-
volver back in his pocket.) Go ahead. *(The DOCTOR*
and NURSE are withdrawing as DALLAS and PONY-
BOY approach JOHNNY.)

DALLAS. Johnnycake? *(He has to swallow.)* Johnny?
(JOHNNY stirs slightly, then opens his eyes.)

JOHNNY. Hey – Dallas 'n' Ponyboy –

DALLAS *(wanting to be sure JOHNNY understands)*. We
won! We beat the Socs. We chased 'em outa our territory.

JOHNNY *(weakly)*. Fighting is no good –

DALLAS. Johnny – they're still writing about you in the
paper. All that hero stuff. I'm proud of you, buddy.
Really proud of you!

JOHNNY *(it's incredible. Trying to smile)*. *Dallas* proud of
  me!

PONYBOY *(as JOHNNY hesitates)*. We're all proud of
  you —

JOHNNY. Ponyboy —*(PONYBOY has to lean to hear.
  JOHNNY whispers.)* Stay gold. *(Then JOHNNY is inert.)*

DALLAS *(softly. Pleading)*. Don't die, Johnny. Please
  don't die. *(His pain is making him angry.)* This is what
  you get for tryin' to help people, you little punk. This
  is what you get. *(Pleading.)* Please, Johnny — don't be
  dead. *(Cracking up. Turns on PONY.)* See, Pony! I was
  crazy for not wanting him to get mean. If he'd been
  tough like me, he'd never have been in this mess. If
  he'd got smart like me he would not have run back in
  to that church. This is what you get for helping people.
  Wise up, Pony. Get like me and you don't get hurt.
  Look out for yourself and nothin' can touch you. Hear
  me, Pony. Wise up!

*(He turns and runs off. PONYBOY goes back and looks
at JOHNNY. The DOCTOR and the NURSE are coming over. As the NURSE starts putting the screen back,
PONYBOY walks unsteadily down front. He's sick and
he's miserable. He gets himself together and turns and
walks back into the living area, which lights up as he
comes. DARRY, SODAPOP and TWO-BIT are all sitting quietly. PONYBOY comes in and looks at them.
SODA jumps up, but before he can say anything, PONY-
BOY tells them.)*

PONYBOY. Johnny's dead. We told him about beating
  the Socs, and he died. *(No one is moving.)* Dallas told

Johnny we're proud of him. Then Johnny told me to stay gold. Then he —

DARRY. We had a call. We know.

PONYBOY. Dallas ran out — all crazy. He couldn't take it.

TWO-BIT *(soberly)*. Even Dallas had a breaking point.

PONYBOY. He kept telling me to wise up.

DARRY *(sharply)*. Pony — *(As PONYBOY looks to him he speaks distinctly.)* Dallas is dead, too.

SODAPOP. We had a call from the police.

PONYBOY *(trying to get it)*. Dallas is dead, too? *Dallas?*

DARRY. He pulled a gun on the security guards.

PONYBOY. It wasn't loaded.

DARRY. They didn't know that.

PONYBOY *(as he works it out)*. Dallas *wanted* to be dead. And Dallas always gets what he wants. *(PONYBOY is starting to sway.)*

SODAPOP *(starting to catch him)*. Easy, little buddy. There's nothing you can do.

DARRY *(getting up. Worried)*. Pony, what's wrong? *(They're ALL looking at PONYBOY as the light is dimming and turning to red. There's the sound of wind blowing, and PONYBOY slowly turns in a circle, trying to keep his balance, about to black out.)*

PONYBOY. The world started spinning around me — blobs of faces and visions were dancing in a red mist. I felt so hot — Then Soda was standing there — *(Calling to him.)* Soda — is someone sick?

SODAPOP *(calling back)*. Yeah. Go back to sleep now.

PONYBOY. Then I remembered — Dallas and Johnny were dead. But I didn't want to think about that — about Johnny, not wanting to die; about Dallas telling me to wise up and then waving an empty gun at the security guards.

(The effect of red and the wind sound are fading into black. Then the light comes up in the living area. PONY-BOY has been lying on the couch and is now sitting up.)

PONYBOY *(calling to DARRY)*. Darry! What's the matter with me?

DARRY. Fever, exhaustion, shock, a minor concussion!

PONYBOY *(confused)*. Where'd I get the concussion?

DARRY. From getting kicked in the head. You've been asleep and delirious since Saturday night.

PONYBOY *(concerned)*. Darry, I'm never gonna make up the school work I missed. And I've got to go to court. *(Worried.)* Darry, do you think they'll split us up? Put me in a home?

DARRY. I don't know, baby. *(Indicating book on the table.)* Johnny left you his copy of *Gone With the Wind.* Told the nurse he wanted you to have it.

PONYBOY *(bothered)*. I don't want to finish it. I'd never get past where the Southern gentlemen go riding in to sure death because they're gallant.

DARRY *(going)*. Get some more rest.

PONYBOY *(turns front)*. The hearing was the day after. Cherry really surprised me. *(CHERRY has come down as did DARRY and she faces front.)*

CHERRY *(this is hard for her, but she speaks clearly)*. Bob had been drinking. He was drunk. When he took me home, he said he was going back and fix Johnny and Ponyboy for picking up his girl. When I begged him, he told me to shut up and get out of the car. He was not himself. He was crazy. He was like that when he got drunk. *(RANDY has come forward and CHERRY steps back.)*

RANDY. Sir, it was our fault. They only fought back when it looked like Bob was about to kill Ponyboy. It was self defense. *(CHERRY and RANDY turn and go off, BOTH of them disturbed but keeping control.)*

PONYBOY. The judge talked to the doctor and to one of my teachers. When he called me, I was scared stiff, but he hardly asked anything. Did I like living with my brothers. What about school and stuff like that. He told me to quit chewing on my fingernails. Then he said, *"Acquitted,"* and the case was closed. *(PONYBOY is coming downstage.)* I wish I could say that everything went back to normal then, but it didn't. Especially me. I started running into things — like the door. I was lucky if I got home from school with the right notebook and both shoes on. I wasn't hungry. Everything tasted like baloney. And I was lousing up at school.

(MR. SYME, a teacher, has come on L.)

MR. SYME *(calling)*. Ponyboy. I'd like to talk to you about your grades.

PONYBOY *(front)*. I used to make A's in English. *(Nods toward MR. SYME.)* Mostly because Mr. Syme has me do compositions. He's a real good guy who makes you think.

MR. SYME. Your grades have really dropped. You're failing this class right now, but I'm taking into consideration the circumstances. If you come up with a good semester theme, I'll pass you.

PONYBOY. Yessir. I'll try. What's the theme supposed to be on?

.. SYME. Anything you think important. I want your own ideas, your experience. At least five pages.

PONYBOY. Like my first trip to the zoo?

MR. SYME *(going)*. If you think it's important. *(PONY-BOY is walking back into the living area.)*

PONYBOY *(as he goes. Talking to himself)*. Well, I know what's *not* important.

SODAPOP. What isn't important?

PONYBOY. Schoolwork! Why all the sweat?

SODAPOP. Take it easy.

PONYBOY. I'll have to get a job as soon as I get out of school. Why not drop out now?

DARRY *(angry)*. You're not going to drop out. With your brains, you could get a scholarship. We could put you through college.

PONYBOY. Big deal.

DARRY *(hard)*. Johnny and Dallas were our buddies, too, but you don't stop living because you lose someone. You don't quit.

PONYBOY. Look at Soda. He's doing okay, and he dropped out. You can just lay off.

DARRY. Any time you don't like the way I'm running things, you can leave.

SODAPOP *(upset)*. Don't—Oh, you guys—why can't you —*(Upset, he goes off into the kitchen.)*

PONYBOY *(startled by the reaction)*. What's with Soda?

DARRY. He lost Sandy, too.

PONYBOY. She's in Florida with her grandmother. She'll be back. They're writing to each other.

DARRY *(picks up envelope)*. This came back today. *(As PONYBOY looks to him.)* It's the letter Soda wrote to Sandy. It wasn't opened. It's marked "Return to Sender."

PONYBOY *(horrified)*. Not even opened!

(SODAPOP is coming back in.)

SODAPOP *(apologetic)*. Sorry.

PONYBOY. It's okay. Really.

SODAPOP. I'm telling you the truth, Ponyboy. I dropped out because I'm dumb. Look, I'm happy working in a gas station with cars. You'd never be happy doing that. You have to understand about Darry, too. He wants you to have the chance he missed. *(Emotional.)* We can't get hacked off at each other anymore. We're all we've got left and if we don't stick together, we don't have anything. *(His hope.)* Pony, if you make it you're making it for all three of us.

DARRY *(sincerely)*. What do you say, Pony?

PONYBOY *(coming to a decision)*. You guys get out of here so I can concentrate. I've gotta theme to write. *(BOTH BROTHERS are delighted with his decision. They're going.)*

DARRY. See you later.

SODAPOP. You'll think of something.

PONYBOY. Something important. *(As they go, PONYBOY crosses to the table. He notices the book and as he picks it up a piece of paper flutters to the floor. He picks up the paper as he did before. Recognizing.)* Johnny's handwriting —

(At the left a bit of light comes up on the only half-seen JOHNNY.)

JOHNNY *(what PONYBOY is reading)*. I asked the Nurse to give you this book so you could finish it — *(PONYBOY is skipping on down till he comes to a part he especially likes.)* I want you to tell Dallas to look at a sunset. He'll probably think you're crazy, but ask him for me. *(PONYBOY continues on down.)* Listen, I don't mind dying now. It's worth it saving those kids. Some of their parents came by to thank me, and I know it was worth it. *(PONYBOY focuses carefully on what follows.)* That guy who wrote the poem—he meant you're gold when you're a kid, like green. When you're a kid everything's new, dawn. It's just that when you get used to everything that it's day. The way you are, Pony. That's gold. *(PONYBOY looks on down the page.)* There's still lots of good in the world. Tell Dallas. I don't think he knows.

PONYBOY (reading signature). Your buddy. Johnny. *(PONYBOY considers for a moment. Then he comes to an important decision. He opens a composition book, picks up a pencil and with deliberation, begins to write. Saying what he writes.)* Semester Composition. Teacher —Mr. Syme. Ponyboy Curtis. *(The light begins to dim out. PONYBOY is repeating the words as he writes them.)* When I stepped out into the bright sunlight from the darkness of the movie house, I had only two things on my mind: Paul Newman and a ride home—

LIGHTS DIM OUT

THE END